PRAISE FOR

Patricia Wants to Cuddle

One of the Best Books of 2022

NPR · *Them* · *Lit Hub* · *CrimeReads* · *Book Riot*
Chicago Review of Books

"A hilarious sendup of and love letter to *The Bachelor* franchise."

—ILANA MASAD, NPR

"It's the best of romantic reality TV competition shows, the Pacific Northwest, and chosen family, mixed in with a queer Sasquatch."

—MEREDITH CAREY,
Condé Nast Traveler

"Who knew a queer Sasquatchian horror comedy could pack so much emotion! As fun as it is weird, which is just plain delightful."

—MICHAEL KENNEDY,
Freaky screenwriter

"For zany surprises, superfun horror and boatloads of queerness, pick up Allen's novel of dating show-Sasquatch-media critique-romance realness."

—KARLA J. STRAND,
Ms. Magazine

"Not one to miss. . . . A funny, eccentric page-turner that you will absolutely love."

—PHOEBE DAVENPORT,
Daily Mail UK

"To die for. Samantha Allen has filled each page with unadulterated, unbridled, unhinged genius."

—JACOB TOBIA,
bestselling author of *Sissy: A Coming-of-Gender Story*
and voice of Double Trouble on *She-Ra and the Princesses of Power*

"Simultaneously lovely and haunting. . . . A delightfully strange and wondrous book, one that takes multiple high concepts and smashes them together, ultimately spinning a story about desire, the things we want, and what we're willing to do and sacrifice to get them. . . . Allen is a maestro of smashing together seemingly incongruous things to make something singular, strange, spectacular."

—KAYLA KUMARI UPADHYAYA,
Autostraddle

"Allen turns her queer sensibilities on the fascinating parallels between reality TV and slasher films, not least their shared obsessions with survival, sex, and the fear of being eliminated. Is *Patricia Wants to Cuddle* a satirical comedy, a horror mystery, or a queer coming-of-age story? The answer is all of the above. In a literary gumbo this exhilarating and thoughtful, our expectations can't help but be redefined."

—PAULA L. WOODS,
Alta

"I devoured it in one sitting. . . . Part satire, part gleeful horror, part lesbian love story, I had as much fun reading this as Allen clearly did while writing it."

—ELIZA SMITH,
Lit Hub

"This propulsive novel is both satire and horror. . . . It also serves as a commentary on consumerism, social media, reality TV, climate activism, and queer survival, while maintaining a sense of absurdity throughout. . . . An enticing mess of contradictions, which is a space that Samantha Allen knows how to fill with ease. . . . If you like the weird discomfort you get from reading Kristen Arnett, or the pulp absurdity of Oyinkan Braithwaite, you will like this book."

—AMERICAN LIBRARY ASSOCIATION'S
RAINBOW ROUND TABLE

"Genuinely funny, surprising, and even—at times—heartwarming. Recommended for fans of Grady Hendrix or Jessica Knoll."

—DIANA PLATT,
Booklist

"What makes a novel like *Patricia* so vital is that it reminds us just how fun literature can/should be, in this case with all the hallmarks of a 'beach read,' that double-edged recommendation. And yet the sentences in *Patricia* are supple and smart throughout, the characters deep, human, growing more complicated as our views into their interior lives and histories expand across the novel."　　　—RYAN MCILVAIN,

Los Angeles Review of Books

"Allen masterfully switches between big laughs, inside baseball knowledge of reality TV, bloody viscera, message-board detective work, and (perhaps the most surprising) a tender queer love story."

—JUAN VELASQUEZ,
Them

"This sapphic novel is a great mixture of horror and comedy that I think all fans of Jordan Peele will appreciate."　　　—EMILY MARTIN,

Book Riot

"This is the lesbian Sasquatch novel you've always wanted. . . . This is the most badass book imaginable."　　　—MOLLY ODINTZ,

CrimeReads

"Allen smoothly navigates the novel's jumps from breezy chick-lit to sharp-fanged satire to gory, no-holds-barred horror. . . . Fast-paced, funny, and thoughtful. Whether you're here for reality-show backbiting, nuanced social commentary, or flesh-ripping monster action, you'll be richly rewarded."　　　—APRIL SNELLINGS,

The Big Thrill

"*King Kong* meets *Bachelor in Paradise* and *Naked and Afraid.*"

—JIM PIECHOTA,
EDGE Media Network

Also by Samantha Allen

Real Queer America

Patricia Wants to Cuddle

Samantha Allen

NEW YORK

For Alexa, the knife in my heart

Zando
zandoprojects.com

Originally published in hardcover by Zando, June 2022
First trade paperback edition, May 2023

Cover design by Evan Gaffney and artwork by Richard A. Chance
Interior design by Aubrey Khan, Neuwirth & Associates, Inc.

The publisher does not have control over and is not responsible for author or other third-party websites (or their content).

Library of Congress Control Number: 2021953081

978-1-63893-051-8 (Paperback)
978-1-63893-005-1 (ebook)

10 9 8 7 6 5 4 3 2

Manufactured in the United States of America

Patricia Wants to Cuddle

Margaret Davies scrubs and scrubs but she knows she'll just have to refinish the deck.

At least the spot where she found the dead sheep this morning. Not that she could recognize the animal at first. The poor dear had been bludgeoned and torn to shreds, hopefully in that order.

By the looks of it, the sheep had already bled into the wood for hours before Maggie, mug of breakfast tea in hand, rounded the corner and spotted the rotting shape outside the sliding-glass door. The sight could have ruined her morning, but one only gets so many mornings, or at least that's what Kathy always said. So when Maggie found the sheep, she simply sat down at the table, sipped her tea, and watched the sated flies buzz against the glass before standing with a sigh to gather tarp, brush, and bucket.

The faint glint of an ear tag under the rising sun was how she ended up identifying the creature: not one from her own flock, thankfully—it was from her neighbor's farm down the road. But it didn't matter whose it was. What mattered was where it had been placed. Everyone on Otters Island knew it had been a bad summer.

What remained of the sheep's wool was stained a deep, almost black shade of crimson except for two perfect white rings around its bent and broken hind legs. The front limbs were missing. *Typical*, Maggie thought, when she noticed their absence. The face had been brutalized to the point that it was no longer a face, really, just a bloody snout protruding from the carnage.

First Maggie rolled the ewe—it was female; she could tell that much—onto the tarp, wrapped it up, then dragged it down the deck stairs, the carcass thumping sickeningly against each step. Crows waiting in the surrounding firs had already discovered the body by the time Maggie finished vaulting back up the steps— two at a time, to keep limber and stave off osteoporosis. Kathy would have been proud, always begging Maggie to go on those long walks she took out to the overlook, where you could see Canada on a sunny day. But Kathy's mornings ran out last year.

At least her wife hadn't died like this sheep, suddenly and violently, although perhaps she would have preferred that to chemotherapy in Anacortes.

On her hands and knees now, rubbing the cedar deck furiously, her left arm aching from the friction, Maggie can do no more. Animal removal will come by later in the day. Word will spread from there. The only decision to be made is when to restain the wood. No point doing it so late in the season, when the rain will just reverse her labor. Then again, waiting until April will mean being reminded of this grisly scene all fall and winter long.

But that was the point, wasn't it? To be reminded.

[One]

CatchChat.com

TRexDerickson · 9.18.19 · 10:20 PM

OK, Catchers. I know it's taken me longer than usual to bring you your week nine spoilers but I *finally* have the scoop on the Final Four. My source in production says the remaining contestants are currently en route to Otters Island, Washington. (Remember how I told you back in July that they were going to film the penultimate week in Japan? Well, I guess they finally looked up the cost of airfare to Tokyo! Now they're going somewhere that has more sheep than people.)

Anyway, I can now reveal that Glamstapix "co-founder" Jeremy Blackstone—a.k.a. America's most eligible bachelor *rolls eyes*— sent home mommy vlogger Rebecca Patton and pharmaceutical sales representative Zoey Sykes during the week eight Elimination Event in Sacramento. That means your official Final Four are: Christian influencer Lilah-Mae Adams, fashion vlogger Amanda Parker, auto show model Vanessa Voorhees, and HR rep Renee Irons.

I'll post a new thread the minute my source comes through with more Elimination details, but if I were you, I wouldn't expect any surprises. Amanda and Vanessa are still your frontrunners this season, like they have been since week two, but I hear Jeremy may be leaning toward Vanessa heading into the finale.

There's only one complication: production was apparently counting on Vanessa to be the villain in the final edit, so if Jeremy does end up proposing to her, they'll have to switch things around. But my source says it's NBD. Villains have won *The Catch* before. Gretchen from season four had a hit-and-run on her record and she still pulled it off, remember?

○ **CatchTheseHands · 9.18.19 · 10:22 PM**

T-Rex! I knew you would never abandon us. Some people were starting to think you had gone extinct (pun intended) but no way were you going to leave us in the dark when they're about to wrap filming. Thank you for these spoilers, but also I'm #TeamAmanda so I kind of don't want to believe you about Vanessa being the top choice.

○ **GlamstaRicks · 9.18.19 · 10:24 PM**

I'm just glad Lilah-Mae isn't making a late-season surge. Anyone else get serious *Children of the Corn* vibes from her Glamstapix videos?

○ **CatcherInTheSky · 9.18.19 · 10:25 PM**

Just because she's a Christian doesn't mean she's creepy, GlamstaRicks. I know it's cool on this forum to hate on the religious contestants, but it's getting old.

○ **GlamstaRicks · 9.18.19 · 10:26 PM**

Umm, *I'm* a Christian? My problem isn't her religion, it's her spouting that prosperity gospel garbage all over social media. Jesus wants you to love people, he doesn't want you to get rich quick selling leggings to your old high-school friends.

○ **CatchMods · 9.18.19 · 10:30 PM**

Moderators here. Let's all be mindful of the forum rules about discussing contestants' religions. T-Rex

dropped spoilers in here 10 minutes ago and we're
already having to delete some comments.

○ **DexIsMyZaddy** • 9.18.19 • 10:35 PM

So the Catch is going to pick the tiny blond girl with the
perfect tits. Shocker.

Renee

The plane hits a bit of turbulence and Renee Irons can't help but picture it going down, the oxygen masks falling from the cabin ceiling like discarded party favors, the screams of the other passengers sounding high and shrill, as though anything could stop the flame from consuming them all in the end. Some people think it would be an awful way to die but the only terror lies in the waiting—the minute or so it takes at high altitude for your oxygen-deprived brain to give up on self-preservation. When the jet slams into the ground, death comes too quick for it to hurt.

"Trash?" the flight attendant asks, walking down the aisle one last time before the descent, jarring Renee out of her grim reverie. "Trash? Trash?"

The man with frosted tips twenty years past their expiration date says it like a question, but as he draws nearer to the *Catch* girls, Renee hears his tone become a touch more declarative.

"Trash? Trash? Trash."

To be fair, Renee has made the same association before. Reality show contestants aren't unlike the two half-empty bags of pretzels Renee throws out as the flight attendant walks past her row: mostly air, empty calories consumed rapidly and forgotten just as fast.

That includes Renee, too, she supposes. Maybe she's read more books than the other girls, but whenever she catches herself feeling superior, she remembers she made the same choice they did to come on this show. Whoever they were before, they're heading to the same place now. Ultimately, they'll all be flattened into pixels and LEDs, reduced to the stuff of sorority house small talk and boxed-wine-fueled internet debates.

Amanda fidgets in the seat to Renee's right, brushing her middle-parted strawberry blond hair out of her face before dropping her hands to her lap. Some empty pretzel bags are prettier than others, Renee muses, catching herself staring at Amanda's nose. She tries to decide whether she was born with it, or whether a surgeon had shaped it into a perfect button, though the answer isn't important, because it's cute either way.

"Here we go!" Amanda chirps, turning to face her, smiling through a bump. "Two more weeks!"

"Well, for half of us," Renee says.

Amanda tightens her seatbelt around the waist of her purple floral-print leggings.

"Oh, girl! I'm sure Jeremy's taking you to the finale. Did you see the way he was staring at you back at the airport?"

Gross.

Yes, Renee had noticed Jeremy's leering back at the gate. This is partly why she half-wishes that one—or both—of the jet's engines would fail, although if she's being honest with herself, those thoughts long predate her time on this stupid show. The other girls might like the lust in Jeremy's gaze. A few years ago, it would have made Renee feel wanted, too. Desire can be such a heady substitute for self-confidence. But she's trying to stop searching for herself in the eyes of others—especially the dead eyes of a greasy-haired gym junkie.

Amanda is still eyeing her expectantly, as if she'd just missed the part where Renee gushed about the Catch. The light turbulence of the plane nosing down saves Renee, mercifully, from having to lie.

"Have you ever been to Seattle?" she asks Amanda instead.

A question for a question. It's a strategy that usually works when Renee wants to hide how she's feeling. Most people like talking about themselves more than they even realize. Renee knows she can get away with only doling out tiny, diet-size slices of herself in her few friendships if she just keeps her interlocutors talking. That's how none of her coworkers back in Tampa know her birthday or her alma mater or that her favorite food is steak frites, and the evasion always works unless the person you're talking to—

"No, have you been?" Amanda asks.

Damn it.

Renee hadn't pegged her for the curious type.

"I've only been once," Renee offers, "but I thought you would have come here for a fashion event at some point?"

"A fashion event in Seattle? What, like a raincoat runway walk? A North Face show?"

Amanda throws her head back and laughs at her own joke. Renee would never tell anyone, and she can barely admit it to herself, but she finds that squeaky giggle sort of charming. The sound of it makes the insides of her elbows feel funny, like they used to back in high school when her history teacher would announce a pop quiz and Renee had forgotten to do the reading.

Amanda probably never did her reading. She looks like the kind of girl who would have copied off of Renee. And Renee would have let her.

The plane tilts down at a steeper grade, then banks right. Through the window just past Amanda's face, Renee can see the Seattle skyline come into view, a thousand white lights blinking against the inky night, construction cranes like enormous glowing crosses filling the few empty spaces between buildings.

"I don't know," Renee says, unthinking, distracted by the sight. "I think you'd make a great puffy-vest model."

Renee feels instantly stupid and daubs away the light sweat forming on her forehead with a napkin. Amanda has already turned to stare out the oval window at the city below them. She may not have even heard.

Anyway, Amanda is the kind of girl who can swim straight through compliments hardly noticing them, like a guppy floating downriver. Maddening how that only seems to make her more beautiful.

"I think I see the Space Needle . . ." Amanda says, her face still glued to the window.

Renee is left by herself to listen to the cacophony of final descent: seatbelts clicking into place, tray tables locking into position, a waking baby crying somewhere in the back. She quickly scans the cabin of the plane, glancing at the young couple holding hands in the row across from them, and giving a polite but dutiful smile to the older woman next to her who'd joked that she always chooses aisle seats because her bladder is the size of a walnut now. Is this all there is waiting for Renee? Love, maybe, and then decay? Her body catching up with the rot in her brain?

Renee turns back toward Amanda and tries to drown out the noise, watching over the other girl's shoulder as the plane descends, slowly—too slowly—and lands not with a fireball but with the dull thud of tires on tarmac, the earth insisting that Renee spend another day on its surface.

Vanessa

The musky sea air is a welcome reprieve from the cloud of Chanel Chance that Vanessa Voorhees has been inhaling ever since she and Amanda piled into the back of the same SUV at Sea–Tac. After living with a gaggle of girls for two months, she isn't sure how much more estrogen she can take.

Shivering, she stares out at the blackness. The others, jet-lagged and weary, had trudged upstairs to the warmth of the heated passenger lounge once the rented fleet of *Catch* cars were all loaded onto the ferry, but Vanessa wanted a moment alone here on the vehicle deck before joining them.

Before her is a rusted rail and beyond it, a moonless abyss. Huge halogen bulbs housed in hazy plastic casings cast a bilious yellow pall over the concrete but fail to illuminate the darkness. Her inner ear and the sound of the 4,000-ton vessel pushing through the waves are her only clues that the boat is even moving. A look around confirms that apart from the *Catch* cars, there's only a smattering of Jeeps and old Subarus parked on the deck. Very few people make the late-night trek to this island, *shocker.*

The eerie surroundings are more than worth the time away from Amanda's yammering. Maybe upstairs she has found a local who's interested in hearing about the difference between Glamstapix's Glimmer feature and ClickClack's Bursts, but Vanessa would much rather stay here and enjoy the dully roaring, reassuring constancy of the churning water.

Still, it would be too creepy to stay down here for long if it didn't smell so nice, like sweat and salt, like her guy friends back home in Denver—a lot like Jeremy, come to think of it, sour and sweet.

God, she loves how he tastes. Vanessa wishes she could be burying her face in his neck right now instead of heading toward yet another empty hotel-room bed. Hopefully she doesn't have a roommate this week. Back in Sacramento, Becca tried to make her stay up late and do DIY gel manicures and Vanessa wondered if she had died and gone to hell.

Only two more weeks, she reminds herself.

Then the other girls will be back home hawking subscription boxes on social media while Vanessa and Jeremy fuck each other in a dozen different countries, and preferably as close to the equator as possible. This boat really is freezing. It's not like any of them would even know what to do with the eponymous Catch if they, well, *caught* him. Lilah-Mae probably wouldn't even blow him, not that the beauty queen is anywhere near as innocent as she pretends to be.

Vanessa leans out over the railing and tries to let her eyes adjust to the darkness.

Soon, she can make out enormous shapes, monoliths hovering in the middle distance, titans lying in wait. Looking closer, she sees that they are cliffs, coastal ones, dotted by hundreds of trees emerging from the crags like bony fingers reaching for the stars. The water slapping against the hull of the boat sounds as though it's trying to climb its way up the deck. And there, skittering between the gray lines of the trees, Vanessa can swear she sees something—a shadow, an animal?—scurrying along the cliffside nearest the ferry.

She leans out farther over the railing, away from the yellow light of the vehicle deck, to keep tracking its movement. What is it?

A cougar? A wolf?

The cold, corroding steel bar between Vanessa and the sea presses into her abdomen as she leans farther. She can almost identify the thing.

Maybe a bear?

With a jolt, the hulking vessel lurches starboard. Vanessa feels her feet slipping as her center of gravity bends over the rail, toward the darkness, toward the water. She yelps as her toes lose purchase on the concrete.

Her pupils dilated now, she sees frothy white caps eager to swallow her. She flails, trying to bend her arms back at an unnatural angle to grab the railing before she plummets into the cold expanse below.

"I've got you."

The man's voice sounds close behind her, and then an arm around her waist pulls her back down onto the deck, which a moment ago was as calm as a cruise ship but is now rocking like a duck boat on a stormy day. In the course of a second, Vanessa's racing heart halves its pace. She takes a step away from the railing for good measure, then turns to greet her rescuer, only to find herself looking at an almost cartoonishly handsome man in his midfifties, his skin nearly wrinkle-free thanks to a readily apparent Botox regimen, his eyes green, his smile bleached-white, and his hair silver-dyed-brown.

Dex Derickson. America's matchmaker.

"Jesus," Vanessa finally exhales. "Thanks, Dex. You just saved me from becoming Shamu food."

Dex looks as confused as his face allows. The guy's had more work done than some of the models Vanessa knows.

"Oh, it's no problem . . ." the host stammers, clearly searching his mind for her name.

"Vanessa?"

Vanessa can't really afford to be offended, not after what he just did for her, but still, they've been filming for weeks. He's met her at three Day Dates and countless Elimination Events, and they even shared a car once in Newport.

"No, of course, I knew that," Dex protests, but Vanessa can tell from the overpowering smell of Scotch on his breath that she's even luckier to be alive than she first imagined. The host of *The Catch* has the same empty-eyed expression as the wax doppelgänger of him at Madame Tussauds that Vanessa once saw while working Vegas. And honestly, the Network could probably replace him with a convincing facsimile at this point because he barely says anything when they film—just empty catchphrases like, "Ladies, this is the last corsage," and, "It's time, Jeremy. Make your choice."

Vanessa's lost count by now of the number of auto shows she's done. The hundreds of handsy suburban dads she's had to dodge all blur together into one beer-flushed pudgy face. But even she puts more effort into her job than Dex does.

The boat leans port and the host stumbles before righting himself.

"I just didn't recognize you from behind is all," he says, too late now to be believable. "Are you excited to go to, um, Marlin Island?"

"Otters Island," Vanessa corrects him, but that's all she knows about it, except for the fact that it's so far north it's practically Canada. She overheard the crew guy in her car complaining that his cell phone thought he had gone international and started charging him for roaming.

"Whatever," Dex says, getting a little surly now. He strolls past Vanessa to lean on the railing that was almost the last thing Vanessa ever touched.

Oh, Jeremy.

God, what if she had never seen him again? Not being able to get him alone these past few weeks has been torture. She wasn't expecting to like him so much and even now it'd be hard to explain why she does, but he's fun and interesting and not at all who you'd expect the co-founder of a major tech company to be.

Dex looks down over the railing and Vanessa thinks about warning him. Did he not see what just happened to her? But he doesn't seem in the mood to be nagged. So instead, she stands behind him, keeping her legs rigid against the rolling of the boat, examining the small bald spot on the back of his head—one that has pointedly never been captured by a camera.

"We almost got Tokyo, you know," the host calls back over his shoulder. "I had a whole spiel about it. I told Network we can get great B-roll *and* great sushi rolls there. But instead, we're here on this . . . piece of rust"—at that, Dex taps the metal railing.

"Yeah, why *here?*" Vanessa asks.

Maybe it's because she almost died, but so far this doesn't feel like the sort of escapist fantasy *The Catch* usually likes to showcase at the end of a season. Usually they go to Fiji or Vietnam, not the fucking North Pole.

"Ha, well between all the tax breaks and local sponsorships, we're practically *making* money filming up here."

Dex doesn't turn to face her, craning his head down at the water instead. Vanessa wonders for a moment if he's going to throw up. How he can hold down his liquor on a ship that's more nausea-inducing than the Disneyland teacups is beyond her. Then again, he's had a lot of practice.

Sad.

Dex could probably still be hot if he still had some life left in him—if he weren't a husk of the more virile man he used to be back when Vanessa's stepmom made her watch *The Catch* with her on Tuesday nights, trying to force her into bonding over mandatory "girl time." She hated the show growing up—never could have imagined being on it. But she also never anticipated modeling to pay off her student debt after going premed only to never go back to school because she couldn't imagine taking out still more loans. Even if she doesn't get a rich husband out of the show, which is honestly close to a guarantee at this point, she'll at least get the kind of boost to her modeling career only a post-*Catch* Glamstapix following can provide.

"Maybe Jeremy and I will go to Japan for our honeymoon," she says, shoving her hands into the front pouch pocket of her fur-trim anorak as the wind shifts direction.

A cold gust blows bow to stern, whistling as it funnels through the entire length of the vessel's open-air deck. Dex remains at the rail, the ship's bobbing momentarily ceased.

"If he can afford it," Dex whips back, almost casually. A slight trailing away of his voice signals to Vanessa that, even in his drunkenness, he instantly regrets saying it.

Wait, what?

Jeremy founded the world's most popular photo-sharing app. He's loaded—in a very different sense than the way Dex is loaded right now.

"What do you . . ." Vanessa starts to ask, but before she can finish, Dex is stepping backward from the railing to stand at her side, his face ashen, suddenly looking as sober as a nun on Sunday morning. He grabs Vanessa by the wrist, wild-eyed.

"Arm," he says, urgency in his voice, pointing at the railing.

"Arm?" Vanessa says. "What about your arm?"

Is he about to have a fucking stroke?

"No, an arm. Water."

Huh? The man can barely form a sentence. He points dumbly toward the sea again.

Vanessa walks back to the railing, hesitant to get too close this time. Looking down at the frothing wake and scanning backward to account for the distance the boat must have traveled while Dex was tongue-tied, Vanessa sees . . . nothing. Nothing but halogen lights above her bouncing off whitecaps below. Maybe he saw a stick or a piece of seaweed—or maybe the miniature bottle of Macallan poking out of the pocket of his pullover fleece is the simplest explanation of all. Vanessa spots the glint of it as she turns around to find Dex still looking nauseated.

"There's nothing there," she says. "Maybe you saw a piece of driftwood?"

"No, it was bloated and, and waterlogged and . . . fleshy-looking. It wasn't a piece of wood, it was . . ."

But even as Dex speaks, Vanessa can see that he's starting to doubt himself. The boat begins to wobble in earnest again. What their fearful leader needs right now is a nap.

"It was probably nothing," Vanessa says, finishing Dex's sentence for him.

"Right," Dex agrees, but doesn't look entirely convinced.

"Right. I think I'm going to go back to my car. I'll see you on Fish Isle or whatever the hell it's called."

Probably for the best. He can go hallucinate all he wants in the comfort of his chauffeured Mercedes. Vanessa just nods back.

"Good luck and everything," Dex says, apparently too self-conscious to walk away just yet. "And, hey, I'm glad you didn't fall in. Can you imagine the lawsuits?"

He says it like it's a joke—but barely—then turns and strides off toward the bow of the deck, his footing uncertain, his legs almost buckling as the boat bobs. Still, he's right. Vanessa needs some luck—just a dash of it. There are still three other girls upstairs to push out before she can be with Jeremy. There's a game left to play, and she's not winning it down here, looking at shapes in the dark.

Lilah-Mae

The Lord has a plan for me, Lilah-Mae Adams mouths, standing in front of the streaky mirror of the ferry ladies' room.

She has to remind herself of that sometimes because it has been hard to keep sight of His will through all the hot tubs and histrionics. Once the season is over, she can get back to the real work of building a worship service for the digital age, hopefully with Jeremy's Glamstapix connections to help launch it. Imagine an entire generation coming to Jesus through the very platform that has led so many—young women especially—to stray from Him. It will be glorious.

But Lilah-Mae is getting ahead of herself. What she really needs to work on right now is her hair. She fidgets with the clip of the extension she could feel coming loose on the plane, trying to determine if it's salvageable or if she needs to ask a producer for a salon pit stop on this Podunk island. Though based on this eternal sailing time, she wouldn't be surprised if the people who live out there used horse hair or something.

She'll get keratin fusion extensions after she wins, of course. Jesus always said he wants his followers to live more abundantly, and Lilah-Mae's abundance is coming soon. She can feel it as surely as she can feel the boat shifting back and forth beneath her, rolling with the waves.

With a satisfying snap, she clips the extension back into place and smooths the artificial strands with her fingers, carefully blending them into her long, chestnut-brown tresses until they become indistinguishable from each other. These darn things are lot of work but her oblong face would look terrible without them—or at least that's what her mom told her when she was twelve, right before her first pageant.

"Don't you look pretty now?" were her mother's exact words after helping her style the extra hair for the first time—emphasis on *now*.

The Catch is a lot like a pageant when it comes down to it. Getting an engagement ring out of Jeremy should be about as easy as bringing home the Miss Dallas–Fort Worth crown was last year. Lilah-Mae just has to stay focused and keep smiling.

Every time she's had to play pool volleyball or go bobbing for apples in the same bucket as a dozen other girls, the residue from all of their makeup swirling in a disgusting film on the surface of the water, she remembers the Bible verse tattooed on her foot: *1C924*.

"Do you not know that in a race all the runners run, but only one gets the prize?"

That prize will be hers. Then *The Catch* can become an increasingly distant piece of her backstory—another part of her past that can be forgotten.

Behind her, the stall doors swing back and forth on their hinges, flapping like loose jaws as the vessel rocks side to side, port to starboard and back again. Some of the hinges squeal as they open and close, their faint howling echoing through the empty space.

Lilah-Mae envies Jesus right about now for being able to walk across stormy seas.

No matter, she has to focus on getting this right. Smiling big now, her teeth seeming to absorb all of the ferry bathroom's fluorescent light, Lilah-Mae speaks forth suddenly and animatedly, as if possessed: "This week on *The Catch*, we're headed to Otters Island, a remote and luxurious getaway in the beautiful Pacific Northwest!"

Was it "remote" or "hidden"? She likes to memorize the promo scripts so the producers put her in more of them. Making their jobs easier means more screen time, which in turn means having to repeat a lot of hyperbole about some truly underwhelming places. What was it she had called Sacramento last week? A "world-class city"? An "oasis of art and culture"?

Lilah-Mae grants herself the mercy of a peek at the Post-it note she stuck to the mirror a moment ago: "Remote." She was right the first time. So why does something feel off?

A clang behind her rings out in one of the stalls. Lilah-Mae falls silent, the hair on the back of her neck going erect. She thought she was alone in here, or else she never would have started rehearsing. The other girls make fun of her enough already.

"Hello?" she calls out.

To no one, apparently. Only the creaky hinges screech in reply.

"Amanda, is that you?"

Frozen in place, Lilah-Mae uses the mirror to survey the row of stalls behind her and notices one door shut, not swinging in rhythm with the rest. Maybe a producer got to the bathroom first? Casey? She hopes to God it's not a local; only a few of them were riding the ferry this late anyway—and judging by the look of them, no, they don't have extensions where they're going.

Lilah-Mae tiptoes toward the closed stall, listening for scuffling on the other side.

"Amanda, if you're filming one of your stupid ClickClack pranks, I swear . . ."

Still nothing.

She leans down to peek under the stall door, holding both her breath and her hair so that it doesn't touch the blue-and-white patterned vinyl floor, which looks like it hasn't gotten a deep clean since the seventies. This bathroom would basically need to be baptized in hydrogen peroxide before Lilah-Mae would consider using it. But there are no feet on the floor.

Just to be sure, Lilah-Mae straightens up and reaches out for the stall door, surprised to find her hand shaking, the trio of gold bar bracelets around her wrist jangling. What if someone did sneak in here to take pictures of her—or worse? Her heart beats harder in her chest. She inches her hand toward the handle and stops short again to see if she can hear any breathing, but the boat's thrum would drown out any sound below a whisper.

"Vanessa? Renee? Are you in there?" Lilah-Mae tries one more time.

But if there is someone in there—someone lurking in the stall—maybe Lilah-Mae shouldn't stick around to find out.

She takes two quick steps toward the exit when a thud on the floor behind her sends a jolt of adrenaline through her already-racing heart. Before Lilah-Mae can whip around, she hears the stall door behind her crashing open. Scurrying footsteps rush toward her. Two hands—strong ones—grip her shoulders, crunching them hard up and into her neck. Hot breath pours down onto her back, seeping through the thin white fabric of her one-size-fits-most Brandy Melville blouse. She tries to break free, but her assailant's grip only tightens as probing fingers burrow unrelentingly into the soft flesh of her arms.

"Jesus!" she screams, squirming, trying to wrench her body forward and out of her attacker's grasp, but the strong hands hold her in place.

Then, they start pulling her backward, dragging her back toward the stall door.

"Help!"

A producer—somebody—will hear her if she yells louder. But Lilah-Mae's attacker only laughs—a husky laugh, but still an alto one.

Vanessa.

The other girl's vice grip comes loose all at once. Lilah-Mae stumbles to find her footing and then turns to face her fellow contestant, furious to find Vanessa grinning wide with a mouth full of Chiclet veneers. There have been practical jokes before, but never any this genuinely terrifying.

"Did I get you, L.M.?" Vanessa says with a snide laugh, brushing an excess of platinum curls behind her ear. "And, hey, isn't taking the Lord's name in vain against your religion?"

"Slapping you would be against my religion, too, but I damn well ought to after a stunt like that."

Lilah-Mae's heart is still pounding, more out of anger now than fear. This girl won't stop tormenting her.

"Oh, Lilah-Mae," Vanessa replies, drawing out the vowels. "For you, I would *definitely* turn the other cheek, if you know what I mean."

Pastor Ted warned her this would happen—that if she came on a show like *The Catch* and stood strong in the Lord, there would be a target on her back. That's why Vanessa likes to goad her and make these little lesbian jokes. Not that Lilah-Mae has anything against gay people. Everyone has their challenges in life: some people are alcoholics, and some people have gambling problems, and some people have desires that just aren't right. Lilah-Mae takes a deep breath and remembers that the world hated Jesus long before it hated her.

I can get through this, she thinks.

She looks down at Vanessa, who only comes up to her shoulders, and probably wouldn't even reach them if her hair weren't so annoyingly voluminous.

"You can tease me all you want, Vanessa, but it isn't going to change how this goes down. Everyone knows this is the week that girls like you get thrown off the show."

"Girls like me?" Vanessa mockingly drapes a hand over her décolletage, which is exposed, of course, in a low-cut knit top. "I haven't read my Bible in a minute but doesn't it say something about not judging others, sweetie?"

"Lucky for you, it's not me doing the judging. It's Jeremy. And once he's done thinking with his flesh, he's going to realize how it would look if he proposed to the girl whose bikini top he took off with his teeth in a jacuzzi. You're blooper reel material, Vanessa. Nothing more."

For a moment, the other woman looks shocked, her lips curling into a pout that seems authentic, not put-on like it does when the cameras are rolling. But then Lilah-Mae catches Vanessa's eyes—glacier-blue irises that freeze and harden in a flash—and she can tell that her enemy has already metabolized the insult and readied one of her own.

"Oh? You think Jeremy would rather fly to Texas and ask Daddy for the key to your chastity belt?"

Lilah-Mae takes a step back toward the exit as Vanessa presses forward, her tiny body taut and curvy like a loaded spring. "'Miss Dallas–Fort Worth.'" Seething, Vanessa takes a plodding step toward her, pausing from her furious gesticulating only to make air quotes. "Little Miss holier-than-thou. Miss 'I'll wear a bikini to win a pageant but not on TV because I'm afraid the religious guys who jerk off to me will lose respect for me.'"

Lilah-Mae stammers, at a loss for words, shuffling backward as Vanessa advances.

The girl's head might be at the level of Lilah-Mae's chest, but a snake doesn't have to be tall to be deadly. All the better to slip unassumingly through the grass and deliver its venom.

"You pretend to be better than me, but you *are* me. You're me with a higher neckline and a crucifix chain. We both want the same thing. At least I'm honest about it."

Lilah-Mae has endured two months of Vanessa's incessant sniping about her religion, her abstinence, her beauty queen days. She has borne it all with the patience of a saint. One night, she even prayed for Vanessa, like it says to do in Matthew. But of course the second Lilah-Mae condemns Vanessa's behavior in the hot tub, their bickering becomes an all-out battle. This is how people usually react when they are shown their sin; it's certainly how Lilah-Mae felt when she saw her own for the first time.

"You have no idea what I want," she says, her teeth set on edge.

"You're right, L.M. I don't know whether you want to *be* Jesus or whether you want to fuck him."

Lilah-Mae's jaw drops.

There are Third Commandment violations and then there are *Third Commandment violations*. If that insult were caught on camera, Vanessa's life would be over. But as Lilah-Mae looks around the drab bathroom, hoping to spot the telltale gleaming of a lens, she finds no candid cameras waiting in the wings, no crew nestled in the corners and crevices.

Even without an audience, Vanessa doesn't miss her chance at a big exit. As Lilah-Mae stands glued to the vinyl floor, frozen in place by the blasphemy she has just witnessed, the little powerhouse of a woman brushes past her—narrowly avoiding contact with Lilah-Mae's now-sore shoulder—and strides off toward the door.

But instead of walking out right away, Vanessa stops at the precipice.

"Oh, and if you *ever* try to call me a slut again," she calls back over her shoulder. "I will end you, L.M. My dirty laundry is already going to be on TV. I know that. I bet you wouldn't want me to air yours, too."

Lilah-Mae watches Vanessa push open the swinging double door and then the girl is gone. Vanessa couldn't possibly know, could she? Even if she did, she wouldn't dare bring that up. They all had secrets they didn't want aired on the show. Even Vanessa. *Especially* Vanessa.

Truly alone now, Lilah-Mae turns to the mirror and waits for her cheeks, flushed red with anger, to return to their normal color. She should try to recite the promo lines again. Otters Island was a "remote getaway," she remembers. "Remote," not "hidden."

But first: mantra.

"Blessed are they who are persecuted," she whispers to herself three times, exhaling between repetitions.

CatchChat.com

CatchTheseHands · 9.19.19 · 12:40 AM

I know T-Rex is always spot-on with his spoilers. Like, I know some people on here even suspect he's a producer. But I kind of find it hard to accept that Jeremy would choose Lilah-Mae over a party girl like Zoey, who looks like she'd do lines off his dick if he asked her.

Why would an unrepentant bachelor like Jeremy Blackstone want to keep someone around who—as far as I can tell from her Glamstapix feed—is still drinking Shirley Temples at age 23?

CatcherInTheSky · 9.19.19 · 12:40 AM

Hate to break it to you, OP, but Zoey already accidentally posted a Glimmer to her Glamsta and then deleted it, so we know she's out. If she were headed to Otters Island right now, her phone would be locked up in some producer's suitcase.

TRexDerickson · 9.19.19 · 1:00 AM

Believe me, I wouldn't agree to be a *Catch* producer even if they offered me the big bucks. My source barely gets any sleep at night and spends all day herding influencers. But I'm quite confident in this one: Zoey is out. Lilah-Mae is in. 100%.

○ **LastCorsage85 · 9.19.19 · 1:05 AM**

Lilah-Mae makes perfect sense to me, CatchTheseHands. Guys like Jeremy reach a point of diminishing returns with the whole bachelor lifestyle and want a "good girl" to ground them. Not saying he'll pick her. (Personally, I think she'll be the next to go.) But she's probably useful to him here at the end, like a booster for a rocket that falls back into the ocean once it's been used up.

○ **GlamstaRicks · 9.19.19 · 1:10 AM**

Does anyone even care who Jeremy picks? Legitimately rich guys don't go on reality shows full of clout-chasing girls whose entire dream in life is to advertise clothes that are so cheaply made they would probably dissolve in the rain. We *all* know Jeremy's angle here has nothing to do with the women. (No offense, Rex, I know a lot of other posters on here are still invested in finding out who the winners and losers are.)

○ **LastCorsage85 · 9.19.19 · 1:25 AM**

Damn, Ricks. Tell us how you really feel. Maybe you'd have more fun over on the *Catch* Stats forum—the one where they talk about this show like it's Monday Night Football. Sometimes it sounds like you don't even like watching it.

○ **GlamstaRicks · 9.19.19 · 1:28 AM**

Hatred is just another form of love, isn't it?

○ **CatchAll · 9.19.19 · 1:15 AM**

I'm with you, Ricks. I could care less about this year's lead. I still can't believe they referred to him as a "tech entrepreneur" back when they announced him, as if he had anything more to do with making Glamstapix than asking his dad to give Scott Evans seed money. I agree with the Catchers who think he's doing more than mere image laundering after catching every STD in Ibiza. The dude must be pressed for cash, too, which means he's going to be in the *Catch*-verse to stay, I'm afraid.

○ **DexIsMyZaddy** • 9.19.19 • 1:30 AM

I swear to God, if he starts another *Catch* podcast, I'll lose it.

○ **CatchTheseHands** • 9.19.19 • 1:33 AM

Right? How can there be so many of them? Are people really buying enough new mattresses to fund them all?

Renee

On the far side of the ferry's passenger deck, in front of a large emerald-and-blue relief map of the San Juan Islands, Lilah-Mae is delivering her little rah-rah tourism speech for the cameras.

". . . a remote and luxurious getaway in the beautiful Pacific Northwest!" Her voice, far too chipper for 2 a.m., rings out across the nearly empty lounge, bouncing against the vinyl upholstered booths and the double-paned windows. "Where blue skies and green trees meet antique stores and local breweries."

The promotional script is garbage, but that's typical for this show. The English major in Renee has given up on proofreading the prewritten taglines and bumpers for *The Catch*. A small huddle of producers and cameramen surround Lilah-Mae while a few locals, tired-looking women returning home late to Otters Island from the mainland, eagerly watch the action from a distance. They probably don't get too many TV crews coming to town.

Renee scans the deck for more familiar faces as she sips her burnt vending-machine coffee from the relative solitude of the synthetic leather bucket seat she's staked out for herself.

Dex is nowhere to be found, of course. He's almost certainly passed out in the car. As of last month, Renee hasn't touched a drink for five years. She knows the signs. Their host is high-functioning when he has to be, but apparently *only* when he has to be.

In a booth across the passenger deck, beside a darkened window, Vanessa and Amanda are whispering to each other. Renee can guess what they're talking about: Lilah-Mae. Vanessa hates the girl, and she's been trying to rope Amanda into shitting on the Christian influencer all season long. Frankly, Amanda seems too stupid to take the hint and weigh in on their grudge match. The only thing that girl feels passionately about are flyaways. It's a good thing she's so damn cute.

And here, off by her lonesome, is Renee, gliding through the darkness at the ass-end-of-nowhere, knowing full well that there's no point even finishing the season.

No one over thirty has ever made it to the end, and at twenty-nine, she might as well be going through menopause as far as the show's audience is concerned. Amanda probably can't even count to twenty-nine without extra help. But if Renee survives one more week, she'll be the first Black woman in *Catch* history to crack the top two—and that'll count for something, right? Or at least Renee had thought it would give her some satisfaction, but on the brink of actually setting the precedent, she's no longer hungry for it. It's not like it comes with an actual cash prize or anything. At best, she'll get her own Wikipedia entry—but having her name forever attached to *The Catch* would be a dubious honor indeed.

Renee has also lost the taste for this coffee, unsurprising because it was brewed by a box on a boat. But if she wants to make it to the bed-and-breakfast before passing out, she'll need some caffeine. She braves another bitter sip and tries to sit up straighter in her chair.

Earlier in the season, Renee thought she might inspire the next generation if she lasted long enough on this show. Maybe she could help drag *The Catch* into the twenty-first century. Lead a horse to water it doesn't even want to drink in the first place. Perhaps it would bring some sense of purpose into her life. At least that had been her rationale.

But it didn't take Renee long to realize that *The Catch* is like a black hole: you can shine light into it, but nothing comes out of it intact.

Over by the relief map, Lilah-Mae has finished shooting the episode promo. The crew members are packing up their cameras. The fluorescent light above Renee blinks off before stuttering back to life after a series of halting flashes. In addition to being as bumpy as a wooden roller coaster, the boat has an electrical system that seems to be on the fritz. Drowning wouldn't be anywhere near as appealing as exploding in a plane crash, Renee realizes. Too slow.

Per the terms of her contract, Renee will have to do a few post-season interviews after this is over. There'll be some minor media attention for the precedent, if she sets it. Maybe she can make a Glamstapix account and live off sponsored posts for a year, as inauthentic as that would feel. Though, in the grand scheme of things, selling tummy tea and gummy vitamins isn't that much more of a scam than running HR sensitivity trainings. Maybe she can finally go to that hotel in Santorini she's always wanted to stay in—the one with the hot tubs built into the hillside.

In the eight years since college, Renee has worked for an insurance company in Los Angeles, then a bank in Tampa, where she made $10,000 more per year and had a manager who was just a bit nicer to her than the previous one. At the brink of thirty, that's what she has to look forward to: incremental raises, glass ceilings, and maybe another cross-country move.

Her coworkers—who were obsessed with the show—had nominated her, probably out of some misplaced sense of white guilt. The casting process that came afterward felt more like something that happened *to* her than something she went through. She told the Network people all the right things like, "I'm looking for a nice guy who wants to settle down," and "I could see myself starting a family in five years," and not, "I daydream about women sometimes" or "I'm not always sure what there is to live for."

For Renee, the show is a lot like this ferry: it started nowhere, it's heading nowhere, and yet she's on it until it gets where it's going which, again, is nowhere.

"What's up, Ren?"

It's Jeremy. Standing over her like a gangly teenager about to ask his mom for lunch money.

Ugh. Where did he come from?

"Hey, uh, what's up, Jeremy?" Renee glances up to find the eponymous Catch, wearing the same hideous neon-yellow tracksuit he wears every travel day, peering at her with that same gross gaze: leering, but without the slightest hint of romantic interest. The foul musk of his hair gel wafts down, invading Renee's nostrils and burning the back of her throat.

"Just exploring the boat," Jeremy says with a shrug. "It's no superyacht, but if you gut one of these bad boys out, build a bar, maybe install a pole, you could have a hell of a time in here."

This is how Jeremy talks to her: like they're bros. Jeremy hasn't even called her "Renee" since night one, when he reduced her to a monosyllable. If guys want to marry you, they give you pet names, not gender-neutral monikers like "Ren" that are also used by insane cartoon chihuahuas.

"Uh-huh . . ." Renee says, unsure how or if Jeremy expects her to respond.

"Mind if I sit down?"

That's not a question Jeremy ever asks Vanessa. He just plunks himself next to her and they start making out. But Renee isn't Vanessa. Nor does she want to be. When Renee made out with him on her Day Date several weeks ago, more out of a sense of obligation than anything else, he tasted minty and yet somehow still disgusting, like Altoids that had been scraped off the floor of a car.

But Jeremy doesn't bother waiting for permission to sit down, taking the green plasticky seat across from her.

"We're not supposed to talk off camera," Renee reminds him, not-so-subtly looking for an escape from the late-night bro sesh.

"The crew have been traveling for twelve hours. I honestly don't think they give a shit."

He's right, unfortunately. Now that the promo is in the can, the crew and producers are dispersing, some heading down to the vehicle deck, others sprawling out in booths by the windows to attempt cat naps in the few minutes before they're scheduled to dock.

Renee spots Lilah-Mae heading over to Vanessa and Amanda's booth, probably so she can pointedly interrupt a conversation about her. That's bound to be uncomfortable, but Renee would trade that awkwardness for this awkwardness in a heartbeat.

"And listen," Jeremy continues, "I'm glad no one's watching right now, because I want to level with you."

He leans forward, elbows on his knees.

Oh, boy.

If he eliminates her before she even gets a chance to step foot on this supposedly "remote and luxurious" forest island, she'll be tempted to spill her lukewarm coffee all over his tracksuit—although, on second thought, not even big brown stains could make the garment uglier than it already is.

"What is it?" she asks him, swallowing her frustration.

Jeremy casts as serious a mien as his fratty, goofy-looking face can approximate, his dopey brown eyes rendered vacant from what Renee can only assume was too much cocaine after college and probably during college, too.

"Look, I'm only telling you this because I care about you," he says. "You've been a lot of fun. I seriously like hanging out with you more than any of the other girls. And you're beautiful. But I can't pick you."

He says that like it's not obvious. Like it hasn't been clear from week two, when he tried to fist bump her at the end of a Date Night. Renee notices him scanning her face for shock, so she feigns a frown. That's the best he's going to get out of her—and even that is more than he deserves.

"I've known since Atlanta," Jeremy continues, "but I didn't want to send you home there, because, you know, uh, you're one of my favorite girls and . . ."

Renee digs her fingernails into her palms. She's not sure which is worse: him coming close to admitting the bad optics of sending her home early, or him calling her one of "his" girls.

". . . and I want you to get something out of this experience, too. Now, look, Dex told me we're headed to Palm Springs after Otters Island for the finale."

"OK . . . ?" she says, prodding him along, hoping this little speech is building toward some sort of point.

"It's a luxury resort. Spa, private pool, everything. So, if you're up for it, I want to take you to the finale. You'd have five days to yourself while I shoot dates with the other girl. I still haven't decided who yet. I just didn't want to get your hopes up if I give you a corsage this week."

Renee could laugh at him for assuming that she would even want to win, but she says nothing instead.

"Of course," Jeremy continues, visibly uncomfortable with her silence now, "you'll have to keep giving the producers good interviews, and say how heartbroken you are when I send you home. Even *I* wouldn't be able to afford this place in Palm Springs. You'll do it, right?"

Renee could get up and storm off. She could tell Jeremy exactly what she thinks, namely that he's a ball of locker-room grime that somehow grew arms and legs and barely learned human language. The exhausted crew would rush over, haphazardly switching on their cameras to capture the late-night fight. She'd tell the whole world how Jeremy has treated her—but without the first part of this conversation on camera, too, Renee already knows how the viewers of *The Catch* would perceive her: angry, overreacting, irrational. She made the mistake of logging on to CatchChat.com a few times before leaving for the show. She knows how these moments go down among the fandom.

Renee experiences *The Catch* in three dimensions: how she herself experiences it, how she suspects they'll edit her, and how she imagines her coworkers would talk about her if she were just a Black girl on the show, and not their "friend."

No, this isn't an interaction Renee can "win" in any meaningful sense of the word.

So instead, she weighs Jeremy's offer for a moment. The ferry's churning and the other girls' distant gabbing fade even further into the background. Hell, she *does* want to go to Palm Springs. If she doesn't wring every bit of travel out of this production, what is she even doing on this boat? She doesn't want to ride this rickety ferry again for a few days more, at least.

"Sure, Jeremy," she tells him, forcing herself to remain poised. His dumb face breaks out into an even dumber grin.

"Hey, thanks, Ren." Jeremy's expression is not quite gratitude but rather what a child thinks gratitude is supposed to look like. "I knew you'd be cool about this."

"Yup," Renee says, draining the last of her coffee, mostly to punish herself for agreeing to this arrangement.

And then Jeremy has the audacity, before rushing off, to lean in and kiss her on the cheek, his dry lips scraping against her as Renee feels the boat slow, at long last, to dock.

Casey

"I almost fell off the ferry," one of them is saying, and it's hard to tell who because when the contestants get like this, their voices all blend together into a delirious cacophony of giggles and vocal fry. The sound is calming, almost, like the chirping of crickets outside a screened-in porch on a late-summer night.

"Was that before or after your bathroom stunt?"

"Before, L.M. After almost dying, the first face I wanted to see was yours, of course."

"Well, I liked the boat. I thought it was cute."

"A tip for the way back? Don't get the coffee."

"Ew, from the *vending machine*? Gross, Renee."

This is the best part of Casey Collins's job: listening to the contestants talk to each other in the car when their mics are off and they can be sure the cameras aren't watching.

For her, it's like a portal into another dimension—a universe where she didn't spend all of high school doodling in spiral notebooks and all of college running the alternative radio station soundboard. These *Catch* girls are exactly the type who would have bullied her back then: effortlessly pretty, relentlessly chatty, and frankly not very bright. But when they're on the show she produces, Casey becomes *their* queen bee—and she loves it.

She holds the keys to *their* futures now. She chooses who gets the biggest storylines and the most Glamstapix followers. She decides who America loves and who they despise. The viewers only think they're picking favorites, but Casey picks for them first.

"Casey, are we taking that boat back, too?" someone calls out from the back of the SUV.

"Unless you want to swim," Casey quips back, sharing a smirk with Mike in the driver's seat. How do they think they're getting back to the mainland? A Learjet? As if the show has private-plane money anymore.

"You're so funny, Casey."

They compliment her as though she's one of them, even with her wavy hair up in a bun and her body perpetually hidden beneath an extra-large UT Austin windbreaker. She knows they're just buttering her up for more camera time, but still. Even tyrants—and Casey can admit she is one—like to be liked. Their forced kindness makes her feel like the girl with glasses who gets made over in a rom-com, but without the anxiety of actually having to get a makeover.

So as the contestants continue chatting about everything and nothing all at once, Casey closes her eyes and pretends for a moment that she's just one of the girls. She imagines what it would be like to have a brain unburdened by intelligence—and then Vanessa's recognizably husky voice interrupts her fantasy.

"Casey, how long until we get to this bed-and-breakfast of yours?" she asks.

For the last half hour since docking at the Otters Island ferry terminal, Mike from crew has been zooming them down narrow two-lane roads in the pitch black, winding past alpaca farms and antiques stores. The car's halogen beams barely penetrate a single layer of fir trees as they round the forested curves. The only light inside the car is the soft glow of Mike's GPS suctioned to the dashboard. Some of the businesses that blur past have seen better days, their windows boarded up, rusted-up cars abandoned in their parking lots, which is a shame because the island itself seems beautiful: lush and green, and, yes, like Lilah-Mae's cringeworthy promo script said, "remote." They really need to find someone with more command over the English language to write those.

Casey is just glancing up at the GPS to check their ETA when Amanda chimes in, her voice high and bright: "Yeah, Mom! Are we there yet?"

"Don't make me pull this car over!" Casey jokes, reluctantly resuming her role as their de facto parent.

She's thirty-two, only three years older than Renee, but they treat her like she's forty-five and taking them to soccer practice. Casey reports back: "We're about twenty minutes away."

There's comfort in knowing their youth won't last forever. The girls Casey produced when she first started working on *The Catch* eight years ago are all either mommy vloggers or anti-vaxxers now, or both.

"Boo!" Amanda calls back through what sounds like cupped hands and the women break out into peals of laughter. It's been twelve straight hours of travel—and people who don't fly every week for a living tend to get loopy by this point. For Casey, this is just another day at the office.

"Jeremy isn't staying at the B&B, right?" Renee asks, trying to make the question sound natural.

Interesting, Casey notes. *He must have already talked to her.*

She reminds herself to check on Renee later, but announces to the whole car, "Alas, my princesses, Jeremy and Dex will be staying in another castle along with the rest of the crew."

Casey knows that a video-game reference is probably lost on these girls, but at least *she* finds it amusing. Sometimes talking to a *Catch* contestant is like speaking to a dog; your word choice is more for your own benefit than it is theirs.

"A castle?" Amanda says, laughing. "You're so random, Casey. I love it."

The word *random*, Casey knows by now, is just hot-girl code for actually having a personality. She lets the backhanded compliment fall flat, like it deserves to. But then Lilah-Mae takes advantage of the break in conversation to pose an obnoxious question of her own: "We're still going to be here on Sunday morning, right? Is there a church somewhere on this island?"

How on-brand.

If there's one thing Casey's good at, it's having information like this handy on her clipboard. In the complicated, many-headed Hydra that is *The Catch*, everyone loves the girl with all the answers. What time does the Day Date start? Where are the Porta Potties? Which contestant is lying about being a virgin? If you want to know, you ask Casey.

"The island is shaped like a horseshoe and there's a beautiful Episcopal church at its center. I found it when we scouted this place online. Very picturesque. It has a hundred-year-old stained-glass window over the altar."

"Episcopal." Lilah-Mae considers the word, as if saying it for the first time, her tone souring further with each syllable. "Hmm . . ."

"What's the matter, L.M.? Are Episcopalians not Jesus-y enough for you?" Vanessa asks, and Casey glances over at Mike to share another knowing smirk.

Mike enjoys when the contestants fight in the car as much as she does, but from a greater remove. When did she last sleep with him again? The season before last? She should go back for thirds. Or is it fifths by now? Maybe he's flexing on purpose, but the camera guy's deltoids are bulging through his Henley as he grips the wheel. He takes a right turn onto another two-lane road, hemmed in close by two grassy ditches, then lifts a hand to brush the shaggy black hair off his forehead.

Casey had to explain to Mike after he was onboarded a few seasons back that the contestants are always too polished when he and the other camera guys are filming them. They all want to look good for the final edit, so they tend to fall back on polite qualifiers and half-apologies like, "I'm sorry you feel that way" or "I can see how you might think that, but I think you're over-reacting." With a loud-enough soundtrack and some shaky cam, the editors can make those filmed confrontations seem intense in post, but it's in fleeting liminal moments like these—on the way to airports, train stations, and hotels—that the girls' claws really come out. It's the reality that reality TV can't capture. It's what every good producer wants to replicate, but almost never can, lightning that only strikes once.

So, Casey has to enjoy these fights while they're happening and hope that they bleed over, in some form, into their shooting days. Somewhere back there in the darkened car, Lilah-Mae's fuse has been lit, and Casey knows it's only a matter of time until she goes off.

"My moms were Episcopalians before they became Unitarians," Amanda volunteers.

"What do Unitarians believe?" Renee asks her.

Lilah-Mae huffs audibly at the question.

OK, here it comes.

"Unitarianism isn't a religion, Amanda!" Lilah-Mae snaps. "It's just a grab bag of beliefs for radical-left grandmas. And Episcopalianism? That's just 'Christianity lite.'"

"Why? Because they accept people like Amanda's gay moms?"

Vanessa for the win, Casey thinks, holding herself back from pumping her fist. *Yes.*

The spirited blonde isn't ready to let the topic die. They've been traveling for an entire day, but Vanessa is still out for blood. She's tiny but indefatigable, like a prize pony. That's why she's Casey's favorite. The girls all the fans end up hating are usually the producers' pride and joy all season long because they create the most chaos.

As Lilah-Mae predictably takes Vanessa's bait, her quaver escalates into a shout, "Look, as the only true believer in the car, I don't know why all of you care so much where I worship. It's honestly sad!"

Casey knows she shouldn't eat this soon before sleeping, but she wishes she had a big bag of popcorn right now.

This is getting good.

Catch viewers think the girls all end up hating each other because of some man, but the best fights have nothing to do with idiots like Jeremy. They're about shit like this: politics, religion, sex, and who's had what done to their bodies. The audience rarely sees it, but the *Catch* girls talk about everything that would be taboo at a dinner table. Maybe that's why Casey loves her job: when you grow up in an emotionally repressed upper-middle-class household, it's invigorating to hear grown women drop any pretense of politeness and go at each other.

"Amanda goes to church," Renee offers, quietly. "I used to, too, sometimes."

But Lilah-Mae either doesn't hear Renee or doesn't care. The car slips forward into the night, Mike grinning at the helm, nourished by the tension.

Casey debates for a moment whether to keep stirring the pot or simply let it simmer. She checks the GPS: ten minutes. Still enough time to help the argument escalate. The angrier these girls get, the better TV they'll make tomorrow. And because they've been awake for almost twenty-four hours straight, the contestants are all primed for conflict. Casey read once that sleep deprivation is still the most effective form of torture ever engineered—and that definitely rings true with her experience.

"One of the cool things about filming on Otters is that the island is a pretty famous LGBTQ getaway," she tells them, as if she's just casually spouting off information from a brochure. "It's the first time in *Catch* history that we've filmed at a gay destination."

Let Lilah-Mae sit with that. Gay stuff is a trigger for her, as Vanessa has apparently figured out. But it's Renee who speaks next.

"What makes it gay?" she asks, seemingly in earnest.

Hmm.

Casey has had a hard time getting a read on Renee all season—and usually she's able to crack a contestant by the third interview. If she didn't need to keep her around for the Big Important Precedent, she would have had Jeremy send her home earlier. Renee says all the right things in her ITMs, with some coaxing of course, but her head perpetually seems to be elsewhere.

"Maybe Otters Island only has sex with other girl islands," Vanessa says.

It's not the best joke in the world, but it's so droll and rapidly delivered Casey catches herself feeling—for the first time in God knows how long—jealous of a *Catch* contestant's humor.

"I've never had sex on an island," Amanda announces. "Beaches, but not islands."

Casey wishes Amanda wouldn't interrupt the flow of all the arguments she tries to set up, but she also can't help but love the girl's beautiful, free-associating mind. The fashion influencer has spouted off some airheaded gold on camera and Casey can't wait to see it aired, perhaps with some whimsical music in the background. Xylophone, maybe? Would a kazoo be too much? Every season needs a ditz. Amanda is actually pretty business-savvy but no one will get to see that side of her. After she got cast on *The Catch*, she started selling branded handbags for $100 a pop that are made in Malaysia for literal pennies. Those are some ruthless profit margins. But this is a game show, not a character study.

"Beach sex is overrated, I think," Amanda continues. "Too sandy. Like, this one time in Miami, I got sand in my . . ."

"Can we not?!" Lilah-Mae squeaks. "I just want to go to bed."

Renee speaks up, out of nowhere: "Lilah-Mae, you can't just decide what the whole car talks about. This isn't a dictatorship."

And then Renee starts to giggle, which reassures Casey. She doesn't know what's going on with Renee, or where that spunk might have come from all of a sudden, but she doesn't want her to come across as *too* sad before getting sent home in the finale.

"Now, please, Amanda," Renee continues, with another chuckle. "Tell us. Where exactly did the sand go?"

"Oh, girl! It went in my ears!"

"Your ears?" Vanessa yells, in mock anger. "Your ears?! I thought this was going to be a *dirty* story."

"Well," Amanda explains. "This guy was behind me. Sorry, Mike, TMI . . ."—but Casey looks over at Mike, and his eyes are glued to the road, staring dead ahead at a straightaway bordered by towering trees on either side—". . . and it's not like I had a pillow or anything so my head was just on the beach. And, yeah, of course the sand also got in my va—"

"Just stop!" Lilah-Mae yells, and Mike slams on the brakes, the car skidding on the damp road. Purses hurtle forward and thud against the seat backs, one of them crashing against the windshield. In a moment that seems to unfold in slow motion, Casey watches Amanda's Hermès handbag fall at her feet and wonders how many sponsored Glamstapix posts she made to afford it, then hopes that's not her last conscious thought. Casey reaches out toward the dashboard with one hand to brace herself, but the seatbelt tightening around her collarbone stops her just short of reaching it.

"Mike!" she shouts as the car continues its slide.

But Casey's cry is drowned out by the sound of the four women screaming in unison behind her. Trees blur past the windshield as tires screech against asphalt. The sharp fabric edge of the seatbelt digs deeper into Casey's neck. The car finally stops and her body jerks backward, her skull thudding against the leather headrest. But she's alive. And at last, the SUV is motionless, pointed at an awkward forty-five-degree angle toward the side of the road, its twin halogen beams illuminating the evergreen forest before them.

"Mike, what the hell?" Casey asks, looking over at her coworker shaking in the driver's seat, his hands clenching the wheel, his gaze unmoving.

Casey cranes backward to check on her cargo, feeling a kink forming in her neck as she does. "Is everyone OK back there?"

"I'm all right," Renee reports, a little shaken.

"I think we're all OK."

"Do you have my bag up there?" Amanda asks, her priorities straight as ever.

Typical.

Mike is quaking in his seat. A moment ago, he looked healthy, happy, and if Casey's being honest, pretty damn hot. Now, there's sweat beading on his forehead and he's trembling, either refusing or unable to blink. "You know Lilah-Mae was yelling 'stop' at Amanda, right? Not you."

"No, I know," Mike stammers at last, some life returning to his face. "I . . . I . . . saw someone."

"On the road? Are you sure?"

The smell of burnt rubber filters into the car through the heating vents. Casey peers out both her passenger side window and the windshield but sees nothing out there in the darkness. The clock on the dashboard reads 3:46 a.m. A pedestrian? At this hour? She doesn't want to accuse Mike of lying but it seems unlikely.

"Who'd you see?" one of the contestants asks, unhelpfully.

"I don't know, OK?" Mike calls back, his grip on the steering wheel tightening even though the car is stopped. "He was walking in the middle of the road and we were going too fast. I was going to hit him if I didn't slam on the brakes."

"Him?" Casey asks.

"Well, yeah, I didn't get a good look at the guy—it all happened so fast—but he was big. And he might have been . . . naked?"

Maybe it's just a release valve for all of the unused adrenaline, but Casey bursts out laughing, the contestants following her lead a half second later. Mike maintains his stony expression, gripping the steering wheel tighter, his knuckles going pale now.

"How big was his dick?" Vanessa calls out, and the laughter doubles, though Lilah-Mae predictably falls quiet.

At last, Mike lets go of the wheel, relaxes his shoulders, and appears to shake it off. "We should keep going," he says.

"Wait," Casey says. "Roll up a smidge and then stop. Let me check the tires."

One thing she remembers from growing up with a dad who talked about his pickup truck as though it were a family member is that long skids can cause flat spots. If there's any damage, she'll want to photograph it for the show's insurance. Network has been getting stingy with the budget for car rentals lately. They've been getting stingy with the budget, *period*, which is why they can only afford a slimeball like Jeremy, and even then, they lowballed him on his fee.

"Don't, Casey," Mike says, but Casey is already out the door, zipping up her windbreaker to buttress herself against the cold.

The rubber smell is even stronger outside, acrid and foul, flooding Casey's nostrils as she steps onto the road. But otherwise the night is peaceful. On travel days, when she isn't wrangling the contestants, Casey practically lives in a pair of noise-canceling headphones. Out here, she doesn't need them. There'd be no noise to cancel except for the car's idling engine, and even that low rumbling is all but absorbed by the trees. She casts a glance at the forest but finds nothing: no naked people playing hide-and-seek in the middle of the night. She walks around the car, kneeling down on the asphalt to check the back tires first. The odor is more intense the closer she gets to them, but there are no worn spots.

As she circles around to the driver's side, Casey studies Mike through the windows with an almost anthropological curiosity. She's never seen him like this. Mike is usually cool under pressure.

When the Catch abandoned the show three seasons ago, vanishing from the hotel, everyone else panicked, but it was Mike who went off and scoured every bar in Park City until he found the guy and dragged him back to set—drunker than he was when they lost him, but still intact.

The tire nearest Mike is fine, too.

One more.

Casey walks past the hood of the car, briefly basking in the warmth radiating off the engine, and then leans down to check the remaining front tire. A chill blast of air comes whistling down the roadway, easily penetrating Casey's windbreaker. Unseen tree limbs all around her rustle in the breeze as she shivers. Any nudists out there would have to be brave to weather this cold.

No flat spots on this one, either.

Before Casey opens the passenger door again, she takes one last glance out into the woods. It's the Texas in her, she knows, but trees that tall have always made her a bit nervous. A forest like that can swallow you up in a way no patch of scrubby mesquite ever could.

She eagerly returns to the warmth of the car, rubbing her arms up and down as she buckles back into her seat. Mike looks relieved by her return, as though he expected the specter he saw on the street to drag her off into the night.

"Tires are fine," she reports. "Can we turn the heat up?"

Mike responds by rotating a dial on the console, but his hand is still shaking. The girls have fallen quiet.

"The guy was real weird, Casey," Mike says, in a low voice that's meant only for her, although the contestants can almost certainly overhear them. "I'm sorry."

"Don't sweat it, Mike," Casey reassures him. Does he think she's questioning his masculinity or something? Mike has nothing to worry about in that regard. After they check the girls into their B&B and get back to the crew hotel, she'll ask Mike to stop by her room.

"Let's just get everybody to bed," Casey says.

Mike puts the car in reverse, fixes the angle, and drives forward.

"And even if there was somebody out there, it was probably just some local weirdo," she tells him, loud enough for the contestants to hear now. "Don't sweat it. What matters is that we kept our beautiful ladies safe, right?"

"Aww, Casey!" Amanda calls. "You're so sweet! And hey, is my bag up there?"

Maybe we should eliminate Amanda next, Casey thinks.

She scoops the Hermès off the floor after stuffing the girl's perfumes back inside, wipes it off on her windbreaker, and hands it back to the contestants over her shoulder.

"Thank you!" Amanda calls back.

"All right, fair maidens," Casey announces. "We're off! Next stop: the Davies B&B!"

The girls cheer.

CatchChat.Com

PNWPrincess · 9.19.19 · 2:00 AM

I know *The Catch* doesn't always pick the most glamorous filming locations for the end of the season. That Phoenix finale was pretty cringe, even though it was funny to watch the girls get progressively more sunburned as the episode went on. But having been to Otters Island, I'm pretty mystified as to why they'd be heading there. My husband and I live in Seattle and we went camping on Otters with another couple last summer. The scenery is gorgeous but apart from that, it's kind of a ghost town. I think it was big in the 90s, especially with the gay community around here, but everyone goes to Orcas Island or San Juan Island now.

GlamstaRicks · 9.19.19 · 2:05 AM

That probably means they can shoot there for cheap.

LastCorsage85 · 9.19.19 · 2:07 AM

Yeah, hotel rates tend to go down when you become famous for missing hikers.

CatcherInTheSky · 9.19.19 · 2:09 AM

Excuse me, what?!

LastCorsage85 · 9.19.19 · 2:15 AM

OK, wow, I'm showing my age tonight but I remember in the 90s three or four hikers went missing there. All of them young women. It was national news for about a month and then everyone forgot about it, sort of like that Malaysian airplane that vanished into thin air a couple years back. People got pretty obsessive about it. Had all kinds of crackpot theories. Serial killers. Alien abductions. Lesbian witches. But mostly it just made people cancel their travel plans. One bad summer is all it takes to dislodge a seasonal destination like that.

Catch22 · 9.19.19 · 2:17 AM

Hope those aliens don't come for the *Catch* girls. On second thought, though, Grays might not even *want* to abduct Glamstapix influencers. That'd be a great way to learn absolutely nothing about human civilization.

GlamstaRicks · 9.19.19 · 2:20 AM

Oh, to the contrary, I think extraterrestrials could learn *everything* about human civilization from Glamstapix influencers.

DexIsMyZaddy · 9.19.19 · 2:18 AM

Some lesbian witches could really spice up *The Catch*. Fingers crossed.

Amanda

Amanda Parker looks jet-lagged AF, so she'll have to get a picture taken from behind instead of snapping a selfie. No one wants to see these gross bags under her eyes. Ew. Besides, selfies aren't in anymore. It's always better to have someone else shoot you. If your feet are in the picture, it means you've got a photographer, a boyfriend, or the coveted two-in-one. Hopefully V's still awake to take the photo for her.

All the other ladies looked like they were near death when the car finally rolled up to the Davies B&B around 4 a.m. Mike's freak-out was exciting but it ended up draining what little energy they all had left after the plane and ferry rides. V's bedtime skincare routine is the stuff of legend, though, which means there's a chance she's up, minimizing pores on the second floor of the adorable Tudor-style house.

But first, Amanda has to plan.

She scans the Davies property from the sweeping back deck, leaning out over the railing and surveying the meadow behind the house. It's so serene here. Even in the dim gray light of the predawn, Amanda can see wildflowers bursting through the grass of the dewy meadow—in September, no less. Far off, at the eastern edge of the property near the sheep pen, the meadow abruptly ends in a neat line and a dense fir forest begins.

Hmm.

Amanda can feel that itching sensation in her brain that happens right before she gets a good idea. It'll come to her.

When Amanda first started fashion vlogging after college, a few friends who took corporate jobs made snippy comments about her work. "So you just take pictures all day?" they'd ask. But her job is just as valid as theirs are, if not more. They don't realize how much labor goes into each outfit, each caption, each post. It's a lot harder than scheduling conference calls and re-stocking break-room pastries.

Take sunrise photos, for example: lately, they've been performing even better on Glamstapix than sunset pics, but that means you have to blow out your hair and assemble your yoga outfits by 5 a.m.—hours before those sad cubicle-bound women are even awake. It's more efficient to take multiple sunrise photos on the same day so you have some saved up for later, but the lighting is only perfect for about ten minutes, which requires a lot of quick changes into and out of tight leggings. Amanda has tripped over bunched-up Lululemons too many times to count.

Today, she only has enough willpower to take one photo—but where?

The meadow is rippling beneath the breeze, as if being caressed by invisible fingers. The air tastes clean, like the entire atmosphere has been run through the air purifier some wellness brand sent her last year. She didn't end up posting on Glamstapix about it—the filters weren't biodegradable, and one of her followers would probably make a fuss about that in the comments—but the thing works wonders on LA smog and wildfire smoke.

The only thing Amanda doesn't like about Otters Island is that the wind moans. Each time it whisks through her hair, a creepy chorus of voices isn't far behind. The sound is faint, guttural and multithroated, like a dozen death rattles happening at once. It makes her skin crawl.

"Sorry about the sheep," was how the inn owner, a Mrs. Margaret Davies, had addressed the noise after they arrived. "They tend to bleat more in the night. They get anxious."

Margaret "Just Call Me Maggie" Davies was a lesbian. Amanda could tell immediately from the Pride bumper sticker on her Forester and choppy haircut, but mostly from her Birkenstocks. In fact, she looked a lot like the younger of Amanda's two moms; her other mom was even more butch.

"Well, Kathy and I never had any kids of our own, but I always joked that our guests were our 'weekend kids,'" Maggie had said, after Amanda eagerly volunteered the details of her own parentage. "So just let me know what shape you want your pancakes to be in the morning. I can do Mickey Mouse."

Amanda's moms had actually been to Otters Island once before. "The lost lesbian Provincetown of the Pacific Northwest." They came in the nineties, before Amanda was even born, but apparently once was enough. Maybe all the late-night bleating scared the tourists away.

The wind blows from the meadow again, bringing the awful sound along with it.

"Baaaaaaaa."

Amanda will have to get at least one picture with the sheep tomorrow, when they're in a better mood. She'll throw on a wool sweater first. Her Glamstapix caption can be: "Who wore it better?" It'll be a long walk out there to the sheep pen. She'll have to go out almost to the trees to take the picture.

Wait, that's perfect.

The long-awaited inspiration arrives in a flash as Amanda realizes how she can frame her sunrise photo: the sun should come up through the tree line at the eastern edge of the property, about a hundred yards from the back deck. She can walk out there and face the trees. In the photo, she will be perfectly centered, in partial silhouette. Her floppy Lola Hat can help hide what all this travel has done to her tangle of dirty blond hair. Then, after running the raw image through a few Glamsta filters, the finished product will have an Alice-in-Wonderland-venturing-into-an-enchanted-forest kind of vibe.

So dreamy.

Maybe the caption can be something like, "Each day on *The Catch* was an adventure." Past tense because she won't be able to post these photos until this episode airs, of course.

At least production gave them these old-school point-and-shoot digital cameras so they can save up content to post on social afterward. She had trouble operating hers at first, but Renee helped her figure it out. She could be kinda sweet when she wasn't off moping by herself, but there's no chance in hell she's going to make it past this week. She's not even on Glamstapix, which is beyond weird. What are you even doing on this show if you're not on Glamstapix?

Amanda wishes desperately that she could have her phone right now so she could check her handbag sales, but mostly to see if she's cracked that critical hundred-thousand-follower mark. She's made it far enough on the show that it's a virtual lock, but it would be reassuring to know that this has all been for something. Jeremy's fun and all, and, yeah, she'll finish what they started back in Newport if they ever get the chance, but an engagement would be a bonus, not a necessity.

With the sunrise picture planned out, Amanda ignores the moaning sheep and takes another deep breath of the delicious, pollution-free air, shivering from the chill. Then, stepping over the weird stain on Maggie's back deck, she reenters the house and tiptoes up the creaky stairs so she doesn't wake Lilah-Mae or Renee. The upstairs hallway is lined with pen-and-ink drawings of red-barked trees clinging to the cliffside, probably by some local artist.

Light is still seeping through the crack under V's door at the end of the hallway.

Phew.

Amanda walks over and knocks, gently. "V, it's me. Are you still up?"

"No," comes the response through the door. Amanda pushes it open, to find her friend sitting at the antique vanity ripping off her own face, her fingers scraping all the way down her cheek in one long, continuous motion, a thin translucent membrane caught in her fingernails. But once V finishes peeling off her detox mask, her flawless olive skin comes into view.

"Didn't you hear?" V coos, not even turning toward Amanda yet. "I'm asleep."

V is already in her pajamas. A Gisele long set.

Nice.

In a momentary flash of envy, Amanda wants to tear the garment off her friend's body. V is so hot that her having nice taste, too, is just overkill. The same designer pieces that Amanda wears to feel cute look like lethal weapons on V's figure. But she swallows her jealousy, as she has for weeks.

"Come on," Amanda whines. "I'm tired, too, but I need a picture."

Vanessa turns in her chair, regarding Amanda coolly with blue eyes that seem to sparkle with bemusement. "Four hundred of them aren't enough?"

She drops her discarded face mask into a small trash bin beside the antique vanity.

By this point, Amanda knows the teasing comes from a place of love. V will ultimately get up and do it, but she likes to be begged. *Wonder why.* Amanda resigns herself to making one final plea.

"It's almost dawn, and we're already up, and I want to get a cool one of me from behind with the sun rising through the trees while I walk toward it. Please, V?"

"Can I wear your emerald gown at the next Elimination Event?"

"The Zac Posen?"

"I don't know what the fuck that means. The green one."

"It's a Zac Posen, and, yes."

"Then it's a deal," V relents, rising from her chair. "Let's go get your picture."

Five minutes later, wrapped in a faux fur coat, Amanda is leading her friend through the meadow that spreads out from the rear of the house. From here, the sheep look like small dark shapes huddled behind a low wooden fence. Chittering birds, sensing the arrival of the morning, punctuate the haunted bleating with their own piercing cries.

"The sheep are still making that sound?" Vanessa asks.

"Guess they're still anxious!" Amanda calls back over her shoulder.

"Maybe Mrs. Davies should try feeding them some Klonopin."

"I took ketamine and Klonopin at the same time once at Coachella," Amanda volunteers. "That was a really weird day."

It was. She woke up the next morning with a vague memory of trying to steal Adam Levine's hat at a pool party—and an entire cactus's worth of needles in her foot.

Amanda keeps treading toward the tree line, her ankle boots sending dew spraying onto her exposed shins with each step. Even with the creepy sheep in the background, this place is so calming. Amanda wishes she could have spent her summers here as a girl instead of out at Joshua Tree in her moms' rusted-up 1977 Airstream. She could have had a boho-chic aesthetic going on—during what would have been the tail end of Otters Island's heyday—instead of spending all of July living in her one-piece bathing suit, sitting in an inflatable kiddie pool to keep cool while her moms drank cheap beer.

Her moms were stingy with new clothes and rammed her through Girl Scouts instead of letting her explore her true passions. By the time she got to UC Santa Barbara, she was dying to wear anything but Dickies.

By now, it's safe to say, Amanda has proved her moms wrong. She's shown them that fashion isn't some "heteronormative" trifle, as they would call it. Not that they've ever stopped asking her what she does for work or whether she needs any rent money. Her handbag sales alone will be enough to live on as long as they remain on an upward trajectory. Well, they *would* be enough to live on if she were willing to move to the Valley, which she's not. But with the revenue from sponcon as a foundation, she can easily afford her small studio back in WeHo.

Amanda slows down as she nears the middle of the meadow. Her friend's footfalls crunch steadily in the grass behind her. She has to remind herself sometimes that she doesn't have to climb the ladder as hungrily as she did back when she only had a thousand followers. Back when she was taking $75 a post to advertise tea that gives you explosive diarrhea.

She's in a good place now. A safe place. *The Catch* will only cement her position—and maybe help her break into that next level, so she can work with even bigger brands. Maybe even White Claw.

"Just a little farther," Amanda calls back to Vanessa. "I want to get close enough that you can't see the tops of the trees, so that the photo feels more immediate, you know what I mean?"

"Mmhmm."

Amanda can tell when Vanessa's being sarcastic. Vanessa's Glamsta, which Amanda made the mistake of looking up during the preseason, is so un-curated. The photos look like they were taken on an iPhone 8—so flat, no angles, most of them candids. But even without trying, Vanessa gets double the engagement Amanda does despite posting less than half as often. The other girl's comments section is thirstier than her own by a desert mile.

"Don't you just love the way the air tastes here?" Amanda asks as she presses forward, trying to clear her mind of jealous thoughts. "So clean!"

"Must be all the trees!" Vanessa replies.

Maybe Amanda shouldn't have offered Vanessa the Zac Posen. The way that gown will bring out the subtle green undertones in her perfectly almond-shaped blue eyes, well that could mean trouble. Jeremy's already into Vanessa, that much is clear, but Amanda suspects she's still the only one who's gotten him naked so far, albeit off camera and only for about five minutes before Casey caught them.

Amanda stops about ten yards away from the firs lining the edge of the property.

"Here's good!" she announces, spinning around just in time for Vanessa to stop short of bumping into her. Together they turn to face the trees.

From this close, they look gigantic, their needle-covered branches swaying slightly in the steady breeze. Shorter deciduous trees compete for space beneath the canopy, and below them a blanket of ferns, their fronds shaped like gutted fish spines, crawl out of the ground. The sky is brightening, but the sun is either still below the horizon or obscured behind the trees.

"What do we do now?" Vanessa asks.

"We wait for the light to be perfect."

Vanessa sighs. "I'm trying to sleep sometime this century. Can't we just use the flash?"

Amanda can only laugh.

"Oh my God, no, that would look terrible, V."

"OK, so we'll just stand here alone in a sheep meadow and wait for sunrise because that's a thing normal people do," Vanessa snarks back.

Amanda decides to let the ribbing slide, counting herself lucky that V was even willing to stay awake for her. She hears Vanessa idly kicking at the grass beside her as she scans the tree line, trying to predict where the sun will appear. Right there, where one patch of trees is getting a tinge lighter than the rest, seems like the most likely spot.

"Can you believe Lilah-Mae?" the other girl asks her. "Talking to Casey about going to church? She probably just wants the producers to film her in the pews. Maybe she'll try to make it into some moment about 'praying for guidance in her relationship,' as if Jeremy even gives a shit about religion."

"If that church is as cute as Casey said it was, V, maybe *we* should take pictures there," Amanda suggests, adjusting her floppy hat and carefully fanning her hair across her shoulders. "My brand is kinda Christian. Like, I'll talk about 'faith,' but not about 'the Lord' like Lilah-Mae does on her Glamsta, you know?"

Vanessa nods but Amanda can tell she doesn't understand the difference. Vanessa's brand is that she's hot. Amanda takes off her coat, folds it carefully, and sets it on the grass.

"I was surprised Renee stood up to Lilah-Mae in the car," V says. "I swear I haven't heard her say more than three words in the last two weeks."

"Renee is sweet once you get to know her but she's shy," Amanda agrees, peering into the forest, still scanning the partially obscured horizon for hints of the sun. "She's not even on Glamsta, you know. I found everyone else when the cast was announced."

An orangey glow appears at the corner of Amanda's vision and she turns to face it—a few feet from where she predicted, but close enough. The sun is just starting to burn through the forest and the effect is stunning. The rays bend insistently around the imposing trees, fighting their way toward the meadow, bathing their ankles in golden light.

"Wow," she hears Vanessa utter beside her, momentarily unjaded.

"See?"

But Amanda doesn't have time to add, "I told you so." It's now or never. She thrusts the point-and-shoot camera into Vanessa's hands, hurriedly reminds her to take a "behind-the-back, partially silhouetted, perfectly centered photo" of her from where she's standing, and rushes off to assume her position at the tree line.

"You got it?" she calls back to V.

"Yup!"

Amanda faces the sun, places her right hand on her hat, and holds her left arm at her side, bending the fingers of that hand outward. The trick she uses is to pretend like she's petting a dog—a tall one like a Saint Bernard. Except there's no dog there, it's just a cute pose that gives you something to do with your hands.

"OK, now!" Amanda calls out.

She hears Vanessa hammering the shutter button again and again so Amanda has plenty of options to choose from later. *Good. She's finally learning.*

Amanda, meanwhile, plays with subtle variations on the same pose: left hand on her hat, right hand out to her side. Both hands on her hat. Both hands petting imaginary dogs. V makes fun of her for this, but it's essential. There's nothing worse than putting in a ton of effort, only to find out later that you didn't get a single photo you can actually use. But she should have one worth posting by now. And it's a relatively low-risk pic because her face isn't even in it.

"Want me to get one of you, V?" Amanda asks, turning and skipping over to Vanessa, delighted to have pulled off the shoot on such short notice.

"No, thanks." Vanessa yawns, lazily holding out the point-and-shoot camera for Amanda to scoop out of her hand. "Come on. I'm going to pass out here in the grass if we don't get back to the house soon."

After picking up her coat, Amanda leads the way across the meadow toward the bed-and-breakfast. The heat of the rising sun cuts through the crisp autumn air and kisses the nape of her neck. The sheep finally stop bleating. Somewhere in the distance, a cock crows. For a minute, the two women don't talk. As they climb the stairs to the back deck, Amanda offers, "Want to see how they came out?" but Vanessa just shakes her head no, walking past her.

"Good night," V says. "Or good morning, I guess."

And then V is gone, stepping over the same stain on the deck Amanda skirted earlier and reentering the B&B through the rear sliding-glass door.

Amanda stays outside to enjoy the fresh air a moment longer. Flipping the camera over, she opens the touch screen to a grid view of the most recent photos and selects the first. It blinks to life on the small LCD screen: orange light wending its way through the trees, Amanda standing there in half-silhouette, hand on her hat, looking appropriately grateful for the day. It might be good to use a quote as a caption instead. Something from Maya Angelou, maybe.

But then she notices another silhouette in the image, this one smaller, darker, and more distant, wedged in a narrow gap of light between two trees. The shadow is so black against the orangey backdrop that, at first, it looks like a section of the touch screen has gone dead, but no. Something is in the forest. Even though it's off in the middle distance, it looks nearly as tall as Amanda, a thick, multilimbed shadow, its edges blurred with motion.

"What is that?" Amanda mutters under her breath.

Instinctively, she takes a step back toward the safety of the house.

Maybe it's a trick of the light or a fly flew in front of the lens. But the shadow looks human-shaped, right? It's so distinct.

Amanda swipes right on the touch screen. In this next picture, her hands have changed position but the shadow remains in the same place. An urgency rises in her chest.

Was someone watching us out there in the woods?
She swipes right again. The shadow is still there. She swipes again. It's still in the same place. Another swipe and, again, the man-shaped shadow is there, unchanged.

Maybe it's just a weird bush or something, Amanda thinks, but it just doesn't make sense: What bush has twin trunks, a long torso, a pair of thick branches bursting out of its sides, and a head-shaped nub at the top of it?

Amanda pauses for a moment, takes another breath of Otters Island air and exhales. The shape was probably nothing. It's not moving—and besides, Amanda would have seen if there were some bogeyman standing right in front of her in the woods. Whatever it is, she can probably edit it out, she realizes, pinching a bright orange section of the image illuminated by the sunrise. Her last boyfriend taught her how to use Photoshop: Just copy-paste this orange part here, drag it over the shadow, and blend. He broke up with her, but she kept the tripod he left at her house, so it wasn't a total loss.

She turns the touch screen back on and swipes right. In the next photo, her hands are midmotion, blurred, on their way down from her hat to her sides. The sun is slightly higher in the sky. The blot of black limbs stains the light. She reaches for the delete button, but something catches her eye. She swipes back to the previous image and then returns to this one.

She does it again. And the shadow's arm bends.

CatchChat.Com

Wow. LastCorsage85 wasn't kidding. Check out this story I found on the Internet Archive from 2004:

May 1st, 2004 (KCRX)

Ten years after the disappearance of three women in Otters Island State Park, family members of the missing hikers are calling on the San Juan County Police Department to formally release all information pertaining to the case.

"We were never satisfied with the initial investigation into their disappearance," Ryan McCreery, widower of Alice McCreery, one of the missing women, told KCRX. "The three-day search felt like a formality—and even with all the media attention on the case, they never did much more than walk through the woods a couple times."

The case drew national attention in 1994 due to the small size of Otters Island State Park and the high experience level of the hikers. Alice McCreery, Kate Choi, and Marilyn Jacobs had hiked the Pacific Crest Trail together the previous year, raising questions and sparking conspiracy theories about how three veteran outdoorswomen could have disappeared in a 4,000-acre state park.

"I think this reflects poorly on Otters Island as a whole—on the park rangers, the police department, and ultimately the entire local government," Mark Richter, an attorney representing the families, told KCRX. "If the original search was as thorough as Otters Island officials claim it was, they should have no problem releasing the case files. If it wasn't, well, that just proves my clients' point."

The San Juan County PD declined to comment, citing an ongoing investigation. The search for McCreery, Choi, and Jacobs is in a "limited continuous" phase, a representative for Otters Island State Park told KCRX. Active searches for the women's remains have ceased but notices are still posted on the park's website.

The number of annual visitors to Otters Island declined steadily after the widespread media coverage of the 1994 disappearances and has plateaued at roughly 100,000 visitors a year.

"Otters Island remains a premier tourist destination, renowned for both charming downtown shops and majestic natural beauty," Otters Island Visitors Bureau president Katherine Davies said in a statement. "Our hearts go out to the families of the three women who disappeared all those years ago. We continue to welcome the thousands of visitors who have safely enjoyed our island ever since."

SOURCE: kcrx.com/s/2004/09/01/missing-hiker-families-demand -justice.htm

○ **DexIsMyZaddy · 9.19.19 · 3:35 AM**

LOL @ that last sentence. Pretty savage of this Katherine Davies woman to just roast them for disappearing like that.

  ○ **GlamstaRicks · 9.19.19 · 4:00 AM**

  I'd be mad, too, if three people fell off a cliff a decade ago and your entire local economy got cratered.

  ○ **CatchMeIfYouCan · 9.19.19 · 4:30 AM**

  OK, wow. Just did some more Googling and there are all sorts of conspiracy theories about how those three women vanished. These are my favorites:

- Apparently Alice McCreery worked for the FBI Field Office in Los Angeles and led some high-profile bank fraud and embezzlement investigations. Rumor has it some shady celebrity killed her and then her friends so there'd be no witnesses. Flight logs apparently showed a private jet from the Burbank airport landing on Otters Island the day before it happened. Some people think Hasselhoff did it.

- Alice McCreery, Kate Choi, and Marilyn Jacobs never existed in the first place. The whole news story was a concoction to distract from a secret military operation. Something about moving stuff from Area 51 to an underground bunker on the island.

- This one's my favorite: Kate Choi's sister, Abigail Choi, apparently *moved* to Otters Island in 2004. She kept a journal about it on Blogtropolis. (Anyone remember that platform? Where you'd pour out your whole soul to the internet for no reason at all?) It was called "Finding Kate," but she stopped writing it or it got deleted or something. Anyway, some people thought Otters Island was governed by a secret satanic cult that killed Abigail, too, when she got close to finding out that they sacrificed her sister.

○ **CatchTheseHands** • 9.19.19 • 11:16 AM

Mods, would it be possible to put posts like this under a separate tag so we can filter them out? Some of us still come here to talk about the show.

  ○ **Catch22** • 9.19.19 • 11:19 AM

  Or better yet, keep this stuff off of CatchChat altogether. Some people might think this is fun, but it's this kind of stuff that starts people down the road of believing that vaccines turn your kids gay.

○ **CatchMelfYouCan** • 9.19.19 • 11:20 AM

Oh my God, I think I found Abigail Choi's old blog. Not all of it, but the Internet Archive still has several of her

Blogtropolis posts. Really fascinating stuff. Who would have thought that some random cold case from the 90s would turn out to be more interesting than *The Catch*?

Here's where it starts:

https://internet.archive.org/findingkate.blogtropolis.com/2004/05/24/marksletter.htm

○ **CatchMods · 9.19.19 · 11:25 AM**

I think we'll cut this off here. This thread is now locked. Anyone interested in discussing true crime can go to Reddit. Anyone who wants to talk about *The Catch*, we can assure you that this is still CatchChat.com.

Casey

Mike is as big as the doorframe and nearly as square. He blocks the light that would otherwise be pouring from the streetlamp outside into Casey's dingy hotel room, with its mottled brown carpet and its over-starched sheets. Casey needs to be awake in a few hours to shoot ITMs, but she needs some late-season catharsis even more.

"You wanted to go over the shooting schedule for tomorrow?" Mike asks her. "I guess tomorrow is today. Well, today is today, but you know what I mean."

God, he can be dumb when he talks.

And yet he looks so good all the time—even when he's wearing this tattered green fleece, which seems to be growing off his body like moss on a boulder. Casey takes a moment to drink in the sight of him. He is standing with one arm above his head holding her door open, his other hand resting on his upper thigh. She simultaneously wants to kiss him and mock him for posing like a pizza delivery guy in a bad porn.

"Yeah, I did," she tells him.

"Did anything change from the itinerary?"

"No, it didn't."

"Oh," Mike says, his face falling.

Does he not get the hint?

"Mike," she says.

"What?"

His confusion seems genuine. *Sweet, this one, but stupid.*

"Mike, do you want to come in?"

"Oh!" Stammering, Mike says, "I didn't know you wanted to . . ."

"I do," she assures him.

And then Mike proves that he can be adroit with his lips after all. He steps forward into the room, reaching over Casey to push the door closed behind him as he does and sweeping her into a kiss once they're hidden from view. She kisses him back, not with hunger, but with the same contentedness of a cat retrieving exactly the toy she wants from underneath the couch.

Yes.

In seconds, she can feel him pressing into her—and that's what she loves about hooking up with Mike during filming. He gets straight to the point. They don't have time to talk about childhood traumas or drink generously poured glasses of wine like the contestants do with the Catch on their Day Dates. She doesn't talk to him about having gay parents like Amanda would, or losing her mom like Vanessa would, or being a Christian in a sinful world like Lilah-Mae would. No sob stories here. She just invites him over and lets it happen. Love is not their leisure; it's their product to bottle and sell. And what's happening between them is far from love. It's more like a perk for holding this ramshackle production together.

This season hasn't been easy. As much as they try to gussy him up, Jeremy oozes scumminess. He's the kind of guy who would fuck girls like Casey at college parties but then pretend not to know her in class the next day. And Dex has been more disinterested than usual, which is saying something. Dex once finished filming a season finale and then asked Casey at the wrap party an hour later who had won.

Sometimes it feels like Casey is the only one who feels the combined weight of the millions of eyeballs they have to satisfy each year. Like if she gave up on the show, it would all just . . . stop.

Casey sighs in pleasure as Mike's kisses creep down her neck. She tries to banish all thoughts of Jeremy and Dex—these two men who together occupy all of her waking hours—focusing instead on more immanent sensations: Mike's chin pressing into her shoulder, his hand gripping the small of her back, his leg stepping between hers. He wants her.

There are more beautiful women working on *The Catch*. Thin girls. Blond girls. Thin, blond girls. Some are even attractive enough that they could get cast on the show themselves, their faces contorted into incessant Glamstapix smiles, the baby fat still puffy in their cheeks. But Casey can nab guys like Mike whenever she wants because she understands them. All guys feel alienated, even the hot ones. Maybe especially the hot ones. They don't want to be sought after or swooned over; they want to be wanted, same as everybody. They want permission to have needs and to be told that those needs are worth satisfying.

Casey just treats men the way she always wished someone would have treated her back in Austin and they seem to respond well to her version of the Golden Rule, judging from the number of late-night hotel room door knocks she's fielded over the years.

In a matter of seconds, Mike is taking off her windbreaker, Casey is pulling off her shirt, Mike is unzipping his jeans, Casey is tugging off his shirt.

"I don't have a . . ." Mike says, looking down at the pile of clothes accumulating between them on the thin-pile carpet.

"I do," Casey says. "It's OK."

She leads him to the bed, hands him the wrapper, and keeps him ready while he rolls on a condom one-handed, like some kind of fucking wizard. That's a new move since Casey last invited him over. Mike has been practicing—and good for him. She hopes he has been cleaning up on the show, just hopefully not with any of the contestants.

Things didn't end well for the last cameraman who slept with a *Catch* girl. An unusually animated Dex made some phone calls after that and now the guy films dog food commercials for a living. It's the worst work in Hollywood: long multiday shoots with Humane Society observers breathing down your neck to make sure you're not mistreating the dogs even though all you're doing is feeding them Alpo.

The firmness of Mike's body brings her back to the present once again. It's easy to get distracted this late in the season, when Dex's drinking is catching up with him. Casey has to keep an ever more vigilant watch over the proceedings. But look at Mike's sculpted chest. Look at how his muscles move and ripple. Look at how the sheer density of him makes their intertwined bodies sink into the too-softness of the hotel's memory foam mattress.

Casey takes Mike into her, and for a few minutes, at least, she doesn't have to answer anyone's questions—except for the one that all guys—even Mike—always ask in the moment: "Does that feel good?"

"Just keep going," she says, avoiding an answer, not because it doesn't feel good, but because the feeling isn't the point.

The point is to prove to herself that she can still attract this type of attention. That it will be waiting for her when she is ready to leave this show. *If* she's ready to leave this show? Casey still imagines herself hunching over craft services when she's eighty years old and the *Catch* finale is being filmed on Elon Musk's moon colony. This show is her home. But being with Mike now reminds her that there are things in this world that are just hers, no one else's—feelings that don't have to be aired anywhere but inside her own mind.

"Wow," Mike is saying, grinning wide. "Maybe *now* I'll be able to sleep tonight."

Casey didn't finish; she wasn't expecting to.

"Why wouldn't you be able to?" she asks, cold now, pulling the sheets up over herself. "Aren't you exhausted?"

"That car thing . . ." Mike trails off.

"Still keyed up over it? It's fine. You didn't crash. We're all alive, right?"

Mike, with his goldfish-esque brain, rarely dwells on stuff like this. Sometimes it seems like you could slap him across the face, and he'd still ask you if you want to go get crafty five minutes later.

"No, it's the person I almost hit, Casey," he says, shaking his head, looking idly at the watercolor hanging on the opposite wall: a painting of a bald mountain ringed with fir trees, a stone observatory rising from its summit like a spear being thrust up at the sky. Mount Resilience. Casey recognizes it from location scouting. They're filming Date Night there tomorrow night— that is, if Mike can snap out of it long enough to hold up a camera again. "At least I think it was a person," he adds.

"What about him?"

Casey is willing to momentarily indulge Mike's certainty that he saw someone—that it wasn't just tiredness and the eeriness of unfamiliar roads that made him jumpy.

"He wasn't just naked, he was also, like . . . hairy?" Mike stammers, searching for the exact right word, as if he's afraid that she'll laugh at him.

Which she does.

"I'm sorry," she says, catching herself.

"No, I'm sorry," Mike says, rising from the bed and scanning the floor for his jeans. "I have to get up early. I'm lead camera for Lilah-Mae's helicopter date."

Shit.

Mike's never been a cuddler, but he usually doesn't bolt like this. Last time, they split a joint and watched an episode of *Frasier* on Casey's iPad—one of those weird combinations that somehow feels exactly right after sex.

"Mike, come on," she pleads, scooting forward on the bed but keeping the scratchy sheets drawn tight around her body.

"No, I try to be chill around you, Casey, because I know that's how you want it," Mike says, putting his shirt back on, depriving Casey of the view she loves so much. "And I like you. I'm sorry. I know you're not interested in that sort of thing, but I do."

Oh, great. He caught feelings.

She thought Mike could be cool about this. Now he wants to be yet another guy occupying her limited mental head space. Mike hurriedly starts pulling on his socks.

"I didn't mean . . ." Casey starts again, but it's half-hearted. She's still searching for a sincere way to finish the sentence when Mike interrupts her.

"No, you laugh at me all the time," he says, his voice raised but still controlled. Even when Mike's mad, he's still so fucking decent. "Maybe you think I'm too stupid to notice or something, but I do. And then you call me over to fuck you, and I try to tell you about that person on the road—and, yeah, Casey, it freaked me out—and you laugh at me? I have an early call time. I could be sleeping right now."

Mike is fully dressed again, his shoulders rising and falling with the quickness of anger, but his gaze remains cast firmly toward the floor. Casey doesn't know what to tell him. She's not sorry, per se, but she also doesn't want him to feel this way. Instead, she lets silence blanket the distance between them as Mike strides toward the door.

But before he leaves, he turns around and, for the first time since they had sex, looks at her directly.

"I know what I saw," he says, then walks out and gently pulls the door shut.

It would almost feel better if he had slammed it.

Renee

"**A**re we rolling?" Casey asks Steve, and then after seeing him nod, she turns to Renee, "So, Renee, my dear, are you excited for another week with Jeremy?"

Renee wants to say she'd rather dance barefoot on broken glass than spend another second humoring that soulless grifter. But instead she thinks about getting room service every day for a week at a luxury resort, gulps down her dignity, and tries to ignore the fact that there is still crusty sleep in the corners of her eyes. Under the circumstances, a wan smile is the most enthusiastic expression she can manage.

She had just come downstairs to sit on the cushioned sill of the parlor's big bay window and take in the scenery when Casey barged in, omnipresent clipboard in hand and a small camera crew in tow, to force her to film an ITM. Renee read somewhere once that vampires need to be invited before they can enter your space. Casey doesn't even follow the same etiquette as Dracula.

"I'm so excited for another week with Jeremy," Renee says, a little flatly.

The inquisition begins.

When Renee woke up, she knew it was going to be a bad day. Sometimes back at home, she can make it to lunch without feeling like she's watching her life swirl down a drain like so much dirty dish water. Other times, she can barely take the twenty steps from her bed to her coffee maker before her limbs start to feel leaden, like they're revolting against being made to move. But this day is bad from the very start, and it's her own fault, too, for agreeing to this cynical bargain.

"Let's do that again, please," Casey prompts, "and this time say *why* you're excited to spend another week with Jeremy."

Renee shifts on the windowsill, turning away from the camera to watch the scene on the meadow as though the show has nothing to do with her anymore, because after last night, it doesn't. A skeleton crew of about two dozen is milling around behind the house, grazing on coffee and sweaty-looking pastries that have been set up for them on long folding tables.

Renee spots Amanda holding one croissant in her mouth while shoving another into the pocket of her coat. On a show full of girls who think they're so relatable, it's probably the most genuine and real thing Renee has witnessed to date. Amanda looks around to make sure no one noticed her but doesn't think to check the window where Renee is being interrogated.

"Renee?"

Right. The interview.

She turns back toward Casey's intrusive setup.

"I'm so excited for another week with Jeremy," she says, the lie growing easier the second time she tells it, "because it's another opportunity for me to deepen my connection with a wonderful man."

That's the best she can manage. Describing Jeremy is like trying to describe the empty space inside an atom; he's technically
there, but for all intents and purposes, he isn't. He's not nothing;
he's worse than nothing.

Renee glances up at Casey, awaiting her next demand, to find
the producer smirking. This is the delicate, circuitous dance they
have done with each other all season: Renee knows that Casey
knows that Renee is too smart for this, and yet neither have ever
said it, instead letting that knowledge hang awkwardly between
them, a frisson in the air. If it were anatomically possible, the
producers would probably rather shove their hands up the contestants' asses and make them talk like ventriloquist's dummies.

"Who do you hope he'll send home this week, Renee?" Casey
asks, leaning forward, tapping the back of her clipboard with
her index finger.

Renee thinks about how to respond.

Tap, tap, tap.

Casey's questions always unfold like this: general at first, then
a little catty, then downright baiting.

Tap, tap, tap.

Here goes.

"I hope when Jeremy makes his decisions about who to send
home this week," Renee tells the camera, "he listens to his heart.
This is such a crucial point in the process."

Turning away toward the window, Renee sees that outside,
Mike and a couple other camera guys appear to be setting up a
place for Vanessa and Lilah-Mae to have a pre–Day Date "talk,"
a.k.a. "argument." Each of the girls are being hyped up by production assistants like prizefighters before a boxing match.
They're both savvy enough to give the cameras exactly what they

want, unlike Renee, who's been cagey in every ITM since week two, this one included.

A producer had told her once that Megan—who went home week three—called her "barbaric" after Renee pinned her during the mud-wrestling date.

"You should talk with her about how hurtful that rhetoric is for Black people," the producer, a white girl who went to Vassar, had said. "I know you hate confrontation, Renee, but you have a responsibility to speak out for your fans who can't."

In response to that particular bit of manipulation, Renee had just blinked. Of course, Megan's word choice was racist. Also, it wasn't her fault that Megan curled up into the fetal position the second Renee trudged into the mud pit. But if Renee had actually confronted Megan, the viewers would have just called her names, too. Everyone on CatchChat.com would be talking about how "aggressive" she was when the episode aired. It was a double bind. Renee had just told the producer, "OK, maybe," and then never said a word to Megan, not even after another round of nudging from Casey the following week.

But Casey didn't try half as hard to goad her back then as she's trying now.

When Renee turns back around, Casey looks angry. Gone are the *dears* and *pleases*.

The producer scoots forward, mere inches behind the cameraman now. The clipboard in her hands is no longer a tool, but a dagger. The nameless lighting guy standing behind Steve moves forward, too, the heat of the bulb causing a light sweat to break on Renee's face.

"Renee, do you want Vanessa to go home?"

"I want all the girls, including Vanessa, to explore their connections to Jeremy as deeply as they can," Renee begins, trying again to be diplomatic. "I would hate if I only made it to the end because the other girls didn't get enough time with him."

"So you think you're going to win," Casey prompts, twisting her words with disturbing ease. "Say more about that."

Casey is treating her like a fish that she's reeling in, but Renee was never on the hook in the first place. She's giving Casey a projection of herself, a hollow persona that Renee has long used, not just on the set of this stupid reality show but in most places: at work, with friends, even with Dad, who calls her sometimes, but only when Stephanie lets him.

At home, she's the same thing she's been on this show. The same thing she is to Casey: not even a secondary character, but a tertiary one, more avatar than human. *The Catch* has only sharpened her façade and forced her to notice how often she hides behind it. But Renee has to keep it up a little longer. She has to play the part she signed up to play.

"I don't think *The Catch* is about winning or losing," she says, smiling big now. "It's about love."

Casey all but winces. The camera guy sets his equipment down on his knee for a quick break. Renee wonders if she's putting up too much of a fight for them to continue.

Nope.

She has only emboldened them.

"Come on, Renee," Casey pleads, her tone ingratiating on its surface but intimidating at its core. "Give me something here. I'm trying to make some television. You get it."

And this is what it always comes down to. Renee has to clap for them like a seal at the circus. Forget looking for love, this is her purpose for being here: to perform. Sometimes it feels like she isn't actually having any experiences on the show—in eight weeks of shooting, she's gone on only one Day Date. A single night that she must endlessly recap for the cameras. But those were always the terms. She's still bound by them and it's Casey's job to enforce them.

Maybe Casey is better than us, Renee thinks. *At least she knows what she is.*

"Fine," Renee agrees.

She looks dead in the lens and ignores the fact that she wants to die a little more with every word she utters. She can keep up this charade, she tells herself, even if it feels wrong to her on a gut level, like letting a tarantula crawl on your face. She'll kiss Jeremy a few more times on camera before all this is over, and swish half a bottle of Listerine around in her mouth afterward. She'll cry—or at least rub the corners of her eyes as if she's crying—when he tells her he's not picking her at the finale.

"This whole experience has been a dream come true," Renee says, switching into the same awful vocal fry intonation she has overheard the rest of the girls do in their ITMs. "To meet a man like Jeremy—that just doesn't happen in the real world. I can't *wait* to be Mrs. Blackstone."

Renee looks away from the lens, instantly regretful, but she can tell from the spark of life flaring in Casey's eyes that the producer got the pull quote she wanted. The vampire has quenched her thirst.

The sun slants in through the window, climbing up Renee's arms, as if scrutinizing her, bringing waves of shame along with it. Renee agreed to this whole scheme, and for what? Money? Something to do for two weeks before getting eliminated? A distraction from the hollowness she felt before this dumb show? Is any of that worth this feeling?

"Now, that wasn't so bad, was it?" Casey asks with a tilt of her head, her voice dripping with the condescending and superior tone that only Renee seems capable of hearing. She gets some sick pleasure out of running her own reality show fiefdom, and her niceness is all surface, sickly sweet fondant slathered over frozen wedding cake.

"Renee," Casey begins, "can you just say, 'I want to marry Jeremy'? Then we can wrap this up."

"You already got what you wanted," Renee says, shaking her head.

"You know it's easier for us to work with nice short complete sentences, Renee. Plus it kind of rhymes: marry, Jeremy."

Renee looks down at the floor, the tension in her body rising until it coils in her shoulders. Maybe she can't do this. Maybe she should have chewed Jeremy out on the ferry, consequences be damned. Her frustration is almost audible now, building into a screech, the volume mounting, the pitch rising until it fills first her mind, then the entire parlor. It sounds like . . .

"Chai or chamomile?" a voice coming from behind Casey asks as the whistling stops.

Renee looks up to find a silver-haired woman in her sixties, wiry but strong, and well-preserved for her age with piercing gray eyes. She's standing behind Casey and company on the edge of the faded area rug covering the living area's hardwood floor, tea kettle in hand.

"Mrs. Davies, we're just about to wrap up filming an interview," Casey says.

It's Margaret Davies, the woman whose house she just slept in. Renee could hear Vanessa and Amanda creeping around in the hallway late last night, doing heaven knows what. After their scurrying woke her up, Renee had lain awake for an hour, listening to the sheep bleating outside, wishing she could comfort them so they could all rest together. In the end, she had only been able to close her eyes for three or four hours before her room started growing lighter through the flowery drapes.

"Oh, I'm sorry," Mrs. Davies says. "I was just trying to offer my guest some tea."

Casey and the innkeeper stare each other down for a moment, evidently at a standstill, until the producer chickens out first and looks down at her clipboard.

"I think we're good calling it here," Casey grumbles. "I got everything I need."

Casey and Steve pack up and within a minute, the lights are gone, the cameras are gone, and Renee finally has the peace necessary to contemplate her tea options.

"Thank you . . . Margaret, right?" Renee says. "I'd love a chai."

"Just call me Maggie," says Maggie, walking closer. "And I'll bring you a scone, too, while I'm at it. From the looks of it, the girls on the show with you don't eat anything besides oxygen."

Renee glances out the window, wrinkles her nose at the dubious-looking pastries on the craft services table.

"I don't need any food, thank you."

The older woman follows her gaze: "Oh, no, no, no. The pastries your crew ordered are from Mary's bakery over in West Bay—and, between you and me, they're only fit to be eaten by the local deer. I made these scones myself. Maple butter. You're having one. Please?"

Renee chuckles.

"OK, Margaret, I mean, Maggie."

Maggie disappears through the open doorway, but raises her voice to keep talking between the clinks and clanks of dishes and cups. Renee stays seated on her windowsill, knowing it would be polite to go help but not wanting to expend the energy after that exhausting ITM.

"So, Jeremy Blackstone, huh?"

"You know him?"

Renee is surprised. Why would a woman Maggie's age be familiar with the hard-partying erstwhile second fiddle at Glamstapix? Otters Islanders don't strike Renee as a TMZ-reading sort.

"Only what I found online when I heard your show was coming to Otters," Maggie calls out. "Big news around here, as you might imagine. He's some kind of tech guy, right? We're really happy to have you here, by the way. Your production is giving a lot of local business owners a boost—even Mary, not that she deserves it."

"Happy to help," Renee says, turning back to look out the window once more.

Renee wishes she were here on Otters to do anything but film more of *The Catch*. What little she has seen of the place has thoroughly charmed her. The landscape, of course, is spectacular: forests and meadows with a gentle mountain rising to the west. And there is a beautiful sort of parsimony to the downtown area that they drove through just before dawn: If you want coffee, there's one place to get it. If you want books, the only bookstore is across the street. It seems like the sort of place where you could actually just live life, instead of researching the best way to live your life on the internet before falling asleep in an apartment full of empty Chinese food containers.

Maggie reappears with a small porcelain plate carrying a perfectly golden-brown scone drizzled with maple glaze. Renee reaches up for it, already salivating.

"You don't sound it," Maggie says.

"What?"

"Happy."

Maggie sits down on a low yellow armchair set at an angle to the windowsill and looks over at Renee with a kindly gaze. The sun pouring into the room reveals an entire universe of dust particles hanging in the air between them. The house is old but homey. Renee realizes this is the first person she's talked to in two months who has sounded genuinely interested in how she feels, instead of just using her feelings for TV. It's refreshing to remember that some people don't even know what *The Catch* is until it literally shows up on their doorstep.

"Let's just say I don't think it's going to work out with me and Jeremy," Renee says with a sigh, taking her first bite of scone.

It's delicious, as expected.

"You know," Maggie says with a sly smile, "based on what I read about him, I think you'll be better off once you get off this show."

Will I be, though? Renee wonders.

This is not where she pictured herself at this point in life, but then again, she had always had trouble even envisioning being alive past thirty. All the possibilities she had seen in her own circles—getting married, getting divorced, raising kids, aspirational suburban grilling—each of them felt tragic in their own right, all equally dead ends. Something inside of her had always felt like it was decaying, doomed, not long for this world. But telling that to anyone would make her feel crazy.

"Are you married?" Renee asks, trying to get out of the hot seat but kicking herself because she immediately remembers Maggie's comment last night about not having had any kids with her spouse, *past tense.*

"My wife passed away last year," Maggie says, her expression controlled and even. Even though the loss is recent, the grief in Maggie's voice sounds old, calcified.

"That's right, I'm sorry," Renee says, setting down her plate beside her on the windowsill, because it feels wrong to be devouring a scone right now. "You told us last night."

"Don't be. You know, for the first six months, I was a wreck. I would burst into tears at the mere mention of her. But these days, I know that Katherine isn't gone—not really. I hear her voice every time I put an extra cube of sugar in my tea or kill a slug eating my dahlias. I catch myself putting out a plate for her at dinner, and then I do it anyway. I don't think of her as being 'dead' anymore, so much as different. Still here, just . . . unseen."

Renee doesn't know what to say. She wonders when she'll ever have that. *If* she can have that.

"I'm sorry," Maggie says, obviously uncomfortable with the silence. "You probably think I'm losing it."

"No, not at all. I think it's beautiful. I just didn't know what to say. I'm so sorry she's gone. And I hope one day I can love someone as wonderful as . . . Katherine, did you say her name was?"

"Well, Jeremy Blackstone is no Kathy," Maggie agrees. "If you're looking for a special someone, though, I'm sure you'll find him. Or her."

Renee's throat goes dry. She had never told anyone that she suspects she's bisexual: not Dad, not the small number of friends she has collected, and definitely not the coworkers who nominated her. She hasn't even used the word to describe herself, though in ways her whole life has been circling around it. It was easy to fuck men, so hard to imagine living with them, and yet also impossible to imagine how, on the edge of thirty, she could ever fit in with people who had known they weren't straight since they were kids. She couldn't picture herself among the throng of loud, proud queers who marched through Ybor City every year. Renee's heart pounds with the thrill and terror of recognition—and Maggie sees her discomfort.

"Oh, I didn't mean any offense by that," the innkeeper says, nonplussed. "We are on Otters Island, after all. We try not to make assumptions here."

"How did you and Kathy end up here?" Renee asks, again trying to deflect attention away from herself. But she also finds herself wanting this kind of connection, craving it, even with an old lady who was a stranger ten minutes ago.

"Oh, it's a long story," Maggie says, a hitch in her throat.

Clearly not one she has the heart to tell right now.

"Well, what a coincidence you ended up here," Renee says, idly casting a glance outside the window.

Out there, Lilah-Mae and Vanessa are sitting opposite each other on a conspicuously placed bale of hay, talking animatedly. Casey has appeared on the scene to order a couple cameramen around. They strafe around the feuding girls in a semicircle, constantly in search of new angles. Watching this scene now doesn't feel much different from that gnawing feeling that has been lodged in Renee's gut all along. She is always on the other side of the glass, watching life happen.

Renee looks back to find Maggie's face crinkled into a smile, her wrinkles finally showing as the sun touches her skin, casting the woman's face into sharper relief.

"I don't think it was a coincidence we ended up here, no," she says. "Everyone on Otters Island came here for a reason."

[Two]

I'M DOING IT. Our mother always told us that we should never expect anyone to hand us anything in life. For some reason, I trusted that the park rangers, the police, the FBI—*somebody*—would call us one day and tell us what happened to her. But it's obvious no one's going to solve this thing for me.

Kate has been gone for 10 years now. Mark's strongly worded letter did nothing, just like I knew it would. (It got him some media attention, which is probably all any lawyer who comes calling is after these days.) The other families all claim they want to know what happened to Alice, Marilyn, and Kate but mostly I think they want a big settlement. Sometimes it feels like I'm the only one who still cares about the facticity of the thing: my sister and her friends were there in those woods—and then they were gone.

Well, it's my turn to look now.

Tomorrow I'm moving to Otters Island.

So as not to blow my cover, I'll be using an alias that I've rehearsed over and over: *My name is Vikki Park. I'm a professor using my sabbatical to do some nature photography.* It'll be the perfect excuse to spend all day up there on the mountain looking for Kate—or at least for any signs of her.

And instead of posting these blog entries in real time, I'll be emailing them to [REDACTED] as a way to ensure my findings get publicized if something happens to me. If [REDACTED] ever goes seven days without hearing from me, she's been instructed to post everything I've sent her up to that point. If that happens—if you're reading this, and I'm gone now, too—I'm urging you to seek your own answers.

—Abigail Choi, 05/24/04

Lilah-Mae

Lilah-Mae is ready to ascend.

As the limo pulls up to the helipad of the small municipal airport—which is really just a sad runway in the middle of a grassy, fenced-in field—she spots Dex and Jeremy standing in front of the chopper. Two black-shirted cameramen kneel as inconspicuously as possible a few yards to either side of the men, with a handful of crew members huddled around each setup.

At the start of the season, it was disconcerting to have a small army watching her go on dates, but Lilah-Mae just ignores them now. In beauty pageants, when a judge asks you a question, you have to pretend like he is the only person in the entire auditorium. You learn to filter everyone else out.

The Catch is a bit different because there are millions of judges sitting on their sofas—and Lilah-Mae has to perform for all of them at once without even being able to see them, so it's hard not to be hyperconscious of the lens floating mere inches from her face.

Mike is filming her from the back of the limo to get a reaction shot when Lilah-Mae discovers the date activity, and that's exactly what she gives him.

"Oh, my gosh!" she shrieks, lifting her hands to clutch the sides of her face, careful not to muss her hair. "I'm so scared of heights!"

She's not. Daddy flies small planes. And she's taken a half-dozen helicopter tours around Dallas with friends. But viewers are already likely to label her haughty and spoiled. She knows the nasty people on CatchChat.com tend to tear into contestants from well-off families like hers. The people on that forum are just like all those people back home who called her "privileged" when in reality her family's money is the result of hard work in the energy industry and abiding faith in the Lord.

For now, it's better to pretend she doesn't even know what a helicopter is.

The limo comes to a stop about twenty yards from the chopper and Mike, his long black hair messier than usual, says, "Hang on a second, Lilah-Mae. They're finishing prep."

Lilah-Mae would try to sneak in a nap if it wouldn't ruin her makeup. She had finally dozed off around five thirty but Amanda and Vanessa's conversation in the upstairs hallway woke her up a half hour later. She had to go beg them to be quiet. In response, Amanda had tried to show her some dumb picture of her by the trees outside—something about a blurry shadow in the image that moved—but honestly, the thing looked like a gnarled tree and she thought they were trying to get inside her head.

It wouldn't surprise her. Vanessa is capable of much worse. Unless she's really provoked, Lilah-Mae has resolved to steer clear of more bickering with Vanessa this week. When you spend too much time obsessing about other people, you're not able to let the fullness of God's goodness shine through you. Plus, she doesn't want the producers to try to send them to a Sudden Death Date later this week. Much better to have this Day Date be her big moment.

Lilah-Mae had a distinct impression that Jeremy would pick her for the activity today—and she knows by now not to ignore the whisperings of the Holy Spirit. The producer's knock on her door this morning wasn't a surprise. She was ready. It was finally here—her chance to use her platform to share her vision of the gospel with the world.

This late in the season, as Lilah-Mae knows from watching the show since her freshman year of high school, each contestant typically uses her solo date like a mission statement to let the audience know what she's all about. For the most part, Lilah-Mae has kept her on-screen persona fun and flirty, but now it's time to light her bushel on fire.

"OK, Lilah-Mae," Mike says, readying a new camera that attaches to his chest and pushing his hair out of his face. "If you just open the door and head straight out to the Catch, I'll be following close behind you. I'm gonna get a Steadicam of your approach."

This is it.

Lilah-Mae nods, pushes open the car door, and with Mike's hurried footfalls nipping close at her heels, jogs out to Jeremy. In his heather-gray T-shirt and distressed jeans, he looks handsome but underdressed next to the besuited Dex, who regards her with the same practiced disinterest he always has.

"I'm so excited!" Lilah-Mae squeals as she leaps into a hug with Jeremy, locking her legs around his body, then remembering that she is supposed to be acrophobic. "But also, nervous!"

"Don't be," says Jeremy, helping her to the ground. "I'm thrilled I get to spend this day with you."

Dex normally chimes in at this point to send them off on the date—usually by saying something cheesy and thematically appropriate like, "OK, lovebirds! Time to soar!"—but instead Lilah-Mae hears some minor commotion among the huddled crew. She turns to her left to find Mike and Dex exchanging a word.

"Hey guys, sorry," Mike says. "Remember that the lavalier mics have trouble picking up dialogue when you hug, so could we do that again? Wait to talk this time until after you're separated."

Lilah-Mae scrolls back a few steps. Then she does her jump and hug maneuver again, pulling away from Jeremy while keeping hold of his hands. Mike swivels around to the other side of the couple, so that Dex will be standing between them in the background of his shot.

"I'm so excited!" Lilah-Mae says, straining to remember her exact verbiage. "But also nervous!"

"Don't be," says Jeremy. "I'm thrilled I get to spend this day with you."

Now it's Dex's turn. Whenever he speaks, the host sounds like he's delivering a radio commercial. He stares directly at the camera, never at the contestants. Lilah-Mae often smells the alcohol on his breath and today is no exception. Noon is early for most, but apparently not for divorced Hollywood elites like him.

"Vanessa, Jeremy, welcome to beautiful Otters . . ."

Mike lowers the camera and interrupts Dex before Lilah-Mae can say something.

"Hey, boss?"

Dex looks pissed. "More mic problems?"

"No," Mike says. "Just . . . this is Lilah-Mae."

"Right. Do we have to do the whole stupid hug jump thing again?"

"I think they can cut around that in post," Mike says. "You can just redo the introduction whenever you're ready, Mr. Derickson."

"Lilah-Mae," Dex begins, taking it slower this time around and acting like he didn't just take a dig at her, "Jeremy."

In the corner of her vision, Lilah-Mae notices one of the crew guys lifting up a cue card. Dex reads off of it, his cadence crisp and bright, his voice betraying none of the grumpiness he displays whenever the cameras are off.

"Welcome to beautiful Otters Island, a stunning gem in the jewel crown that is the Pacific Northwest. We wanted you both to take your love to new heights today, so we've arranged for Peregrine Tours to take you on a private helicopter ride around the entire island. Are you both ready for adventure?"

"I think we are, Dex!" Lilah-Mae responds with the sort of feigned enthusiasm she knows they're looking for as Jeremy nods in agreement.

"Great!" Dex says, somehow managing to sound both enthusiastic and dead inside at the same time. "Then fly safe, you two, and I'll see you both at Date Night."

The helicopter pilot, his eyes obscured by the face shield of his helmet, emerges from the vehicle on cue to help Lilah-Mae, Jeremy, and Mike onboard. But as she climbs up, Lilah-Mae can hear Dex muttering to the cue-card guy.

"'Gem in the jewel crown'? Really? Who's writing this shit?"

"Do everything without grumbling," Paul once wrote to the Philippians—words Dex *definitely* didn't live by. They're also words Lilah-Mae's stomach isn't living by as she struggles to digest the pancakes that lady-loving innkeeper made for her this morning.

But then the helicopter door is sliding closed, Mike is handing them both over-ear headsets, and Lilah-Mae has to shake off Dex's negativity to focus on her purpose. She and Jeremy sit beside each other in the back of the chopper, with Mike strapped in opposite them, holding the camera threateningly close to their faces. What that lens witnesses for the next few minutes will be far more important than what Jeremy sees.

"Everybody ready to fly back there?" the pilot's voice comes crackling through the headset.

"All set, chief," Mike tells him.

The rotors whir and accelerate. Lilah-Mae's headset barely muffles the noise, but when Jeremy speaks, his voice gets piped into her ears, cutting through the deafening whir of the blades. "You said you were nervous. Have you ever been on a helicopter before?"

"No, only planes," she lies.

"Well, they're a little bumpier than airplanes," Jeremy says. "Like, this one time in the Swiss Alps . . . well, I'll tell you that story sometime when you're not on your first chopper ride."

The helicopter lifts off the ground with a jerk and Lilah-Mae yelps from the g-force that glues her butt to the seat. She is now—genuinely—a little scared. This pilot is flying more aggressively than the ones who usually take her and her pageant friends on skyline tours of Dallas.

"Don't worry about your life," Lilah-Mae whispers, remembering too late that her headset plays whatever she says directly into everyone else's ears.

"What's that?" Jeremy asks her, as the chopper pulls above the evergreen trees that seemed almost insurmountably high when they were on the ground. What a difference a little perspective makes. There's a lesson in there somewhere. Maybe even a sermon.

"Oh, it's from Luke," Lilah-Mae tells him, catching Jeremy's muddy brown eyes with her own, doing her best to keep it casual. "I say it sometimes when I'm scared. It's Jesus telling his followers that life is more than just our bodies. 'Life is more than food, and the body more than clothes.'"

"Better not tell Amanda that last part," Jeremy jokes, and Lilah-Mae can't help but giggle, though she knows that won't play well on camera. The other girls can be as catty as they want, but when a Christian tries to get in on the fun, too, all of a sudden she's branded a hypocrite.

As the helicopter soars above the tree line and tilts toward the sea, Lilah-Mae turns to the window and sees the beauty of God's creation in all its splendor: Sunlight made on the first day pours down onto cobalt seas that were made on the second. The island's farms and meadows look like little green postage stamps pasted among the verdant swaths of even greener forest.

How could anyone look at this sight and think that it had happened randomly with no grand design? Was it any wonder that God looked at what he made and called it "good"?

"Your faith seems really important to you, Lilah-Mae," Jeremy says, following her gaze out the window, seeming to notice the reverence in her face.

"It is," Lilah-Mae confirms.

She wasn't planning on helicopter turbulence being the catalyst for this conversation, but she did want to have it on this date somehow, in the unlikely event this ends up being her last stretch of uninterrupted screen time on *The Catch*.

"Yeah, faith is important to me, too," Jeremy tells her, and either the headset glitched or his voice broke partway through the sentence.

Interesting.

This wasn't the response Lilah-Mae was expecting. She's not dumb. She knows Jeremy has been partying ever since he cashed out his Glamstapix shares. Even Pastor Ted back home had seen the tabloid headlines about his parties in San Francisco. Something about a potato cannon filled with cocaine? Jeremy has been more image-conscious these days, which is why she knows he'll never propose to Vanessa. He's done with that kind of girl, surely. But is he really trying to tell her that he wants to be born again? Lilah-Mae knows firsthand it's possible to change through Christ, but Jeremy has *a lot* of changing to do, especially after doing body shots off of Zoey the same week he sent her home.

"Can you tell me more about your faith?" Lilah-Mae asks.

The helicopter swoops to the right, and Lilah-Mae swallows down some motion sickness. Daddy's planes encountered turbulence, but they never careened this suddenly. The pilot is flying like he's got a schedule to keep. Even Mike, who must have filmed countless helicopter dates by now, is anxiously gripping his seat with one hand while holding up his camera with a single bulging arm.

Lilah-Mae looks past Mike to glare at the pilot, only to find him pointing out a low-lying, fir-covered mountain coming into view through the windshield. A single road doubles back on itself a dozen times as it climbs toward the summit. The peak is bald stone, an old observatory at its center surrounded by a sparse scattering of bare trees. The mountain looks like a dead eye, the road jagged like a burst blood vessel emanating from a listless gray iris. Maybe it's nausea, but Lilah-Mae feels a weird sense of unease at the sight of it.

"Mount Resilience," the pilot announces.

"We're filming Date Night there," Mike whispers through his headset, while making a circular motion at Jeremy and Lilah-Mae to indicate they should keep rolling. Lilah-Mae has lost the thread of their conversation, but the Catch is unfazed by the interruption.

"Look, I don't think it's any secret that I got wild after I left the Glamstapix board—and maybe I'm still a little wild," he says with a laugh. "But I've realized there's more to life than money, mansions, and women."

He couldn't have teed up Lilah-Mae more perfectly. This is her chance to share her message. It doesn't matter if she buys Jeremy's transformation, which she doesn't—at least not yet. She isn't talking to Jeremy now; she's speaking to millions of *Catch* viewers. She collects herself, remembers her bullet points, and begins the speech she hopes the editors will air relatively intact. If the pilot keeps flying like he does, they could end up being her last words anyway.

"I think that's so important," she says, interlacing her hand with Jeremy's. "I mean, I believe the Lord wants us to have prosperity and abundance, but it's about what you use it for, you know?"

The helicopter lurches left and Lilah-Mae feels the motion with her whole body, almost like her internal organs are shifting position a few seconds behind her skeleton, but she rallies. She needs to get enough of her speech out that, even if they edit her down, her message can still be transmitted to the viewers at home. She forgets the churning in her stomach and shares some wisdom from above.

"Paul said in Second Corinthians that God blesses us abundantly so that we can abound in good works. I've been blessed in my life to be raised in a good family and to win Miss Dallas–Fort Worth, and now I'm just trying to share some of those blessings with the world. I think that's what Jesus would want me to do, and I'm just grateful I have the opportunity to do it."

Phew.

Jeremy gives her hand a squeeze of acknowledgment and leans in to kiss her.

"That's beautiful," he says, his lips inching closer to hers.

"You can see the whole island now," the pilot says, his face shield pointed forward, seemingly unaware that he is ruining a perfect TV moment.

A frustrated Lilah-Mae turns to her side window, looking down at the horseshoe-shaped island below her, Mount Resilience on the west side, tree-lined limestone cliffs on the east. She squints to see if she can spot the church that Casey mentioned in the car last night, but as she shifts her focus, her stomach roils and her head swims and then Lilah-Mae is no longer looking at the island but at her own breakfast as it splatters onto the window.

"Shit," she utters without thinking.

Mortified, she fumbles for anything she can use to wipe her face while staying as hidden from Mike's probing camera as she can.

No, no, no.

"Are you OK?" Jeremy's voice comes crackling through her headset.

Turning slightly, she notices the pilot handing Mike a gallon-size plastic baggie with a packet of pills, a small bottle of water, and a washcloth.

"Sorry about that, hon," the pilot's voice crackles. "I meant to distribute these before liftoff."

Jeremy grabs the nausea kit from Mike, pulls out the wash-cloth, and hands it to Lilah-Mae, who blots her face with the coarse fabric, angling away from the camera, which is still roll-ing, of course. There's no way they won't air this moment.

"Don't worry," Jeremy says, placing a hand on her shoulder like he's comforting a sick farm animal. But there's a quaver in his voice. The careening of the chopper must have rattled him, too.

Did they hire the worst helicopter pilot in the world on purpose?

Her face finally as clean as she can get it without having ac-cess to a sink, Lilah-Mae turns to face the men. That's when she sees Mike, trying and failing to suppress a smile, clearly pleased with what he has caught on film—and she knows for certain now that her entire speech was for naught. What could have been her big moment—her light shining from atop a hill—is now going to be replaced with her throwing up and then imme-diately getting bleeped after making a point of not swearing all season.

It'll probably even end up in the promo.

Pastor Ted said they would try to snare her like this. He pre-dicted they would lay traps to undercut and deflate her. The day before she left for the show, he even called her and told her the Spirit had told him she shouldn't go. Maybe she should have listened to that still, small voice.

"You OK?" Jeremy asks again, rubbing her back, a kiss now clearly the last thing on his mind.

Lilah-Mae would like to go back down now.

OTTERS ISLAND DOESN'T look sinister at first glance. Not at all like the sort of place that covered up my sister's disappearance. Because the Olympic Mountains block the rain, the sunlight here is spectacular, almost sanitizing, as if it's desperate to convince you that this town is all surface and no shadows. The madrona trees compete for space on the limestone cliffs, like they've all dared each other to get as close as they can get to the water without sliding off the edge into the sea. The beauty only adds to the deception.

What's left of the small downtown is dated but charming: a coffee shop that mostly serves locals, a hotel right on the water, a row of antique shops and art galleries with prices that only tourists would pay, if there were any. I can see why Kate and her friends chose to come to Otters, trading in one of their usual punishing wilderness treks for moderate trails and quainter pleasures. You could have a very nice weekend here if you weren't looking for ghosts.

When I checked into the hotel last night, I told the concierge that I would be staying here for a while and she replied with a fake smile that small islands are sometimes the best places to make big changes. Sounded like something you'd embroider on a throw pillow.

She told me that too few people are moving here these days. I could have pressed her but I didn't. Too soon. I can't risk raising their suspicions just yet.

First, I want to retrace Kate's footsteps. We know that they parked by the lake midway up Mount Resilience. And thanks to the marked-up map one of them left behind in the car (not Kate's handwriting—maybe Marilyn's?), I know what path they took: first, a loop around the lake and then a steep climb to the summit before doubling back and walking down to the parking area. Except they never made it back to the car. Not that anyone on this damned island seemed to care.

I'm under no illusion that I'll find Kate herself after all these years, though at this point anything is possible. But her carabiners, her boots, *something*, should still be out here somewhere.

I'm not leaving until I figure out what happened to her.

—Abigail Choi 06/02/04

Vanessa

Most of *The Catch* is waiting. During the audition process, no one tells you just how much time you're going to spend sitting on your ass, doing nothing, or getting driven around, like Vanessa is now, sitting alone in the back of a Lincoln Town Car headed toward Mount Resilience.

It's a nice sedan—a classic for good reason—with leather upholstery and a soundproof sliding-glass partition between her and the front seat, where Casey is pointing out the next turn ahead to Mike. Their lips are moving, but she can't hear a word, which is honestly fucking fantastic. Usually, the producers don't shut up, always bugging Vanessa to do ITMs and asking her how she's feeling, but they like to keep her and the other girls in the closest thing they can get to solitary confinement before Date Nights.

As Mike takes the left, a slate-blue lake comes into view through Vanessa's side window. The ride is smooth—much smoother than the last time Mike drove them. Maybe he's better in a car with a lower center of gravity, which is lucky because Town Cars cling to the ground like they're afraid of flying.

Vanessa almost did a little work for Lincoln once. They're cars for old people but they like their models young.

"You're not just a model; you're a product specialist," the casting agent told her, and sure, Vanessa knows a lot about each car she's stood next to, but let's be real, she knows what the most important part of her job is. Unlike some contestants on this show, she's able to be honest about what she uses her body for.

Through the windshield, there's another identical Town Car and through the rear window, yet another. L.M.'s in one of them, probably saying a prayer for a good Date Night or quaking in her boots hoping Vanessa doesn't share what she knows.

Amanda's likely sitting in the back of her sedan, Vanessa decides, brushing her hair or contouring or whatever weird little smoke-and-mirrors trick she thinks will make Jeremy like her more, as if he gives a shit about where she parts her hair. Amanda spends so much time trying to look pretty and successful for a following of mostly teenage girls on Glamstapix. Does she even want to *fuck* a man? Sometimes it seems like she'd be just as happy with a cardboard cutout for a boyfriend if he looked real enough in pictures.

The only girl in the Final Four she hasn't figured out yet is Renee. Quiet Renee. But you have to watch out for the quiet ones.

Vanessa's strategy session is interrupted by low fuzzy static, barely noticeable above the sound of the tires. It takes her a second to locate the source: a small speaker below the partition near the rear cabin A/C controls. She's seen this on some custom jobs before: a soundproof partition with an intercom, so that the rich guys who typically get carted around in these things can still yell at their drivers whenever they want to.

"It's short for 'glamorous camping,'" Casey's voice comes crackling over the intercom.

Vanessa, baffled by the interjection, is about to respond when she realizes the producer isn't even talking to her but into her phone, which she's holding out in front of her chin. She must be leaning on the intercom button or something without realizing it.

"'Glamping,' huh?" a fainter but still recognizable voice responds.

Dex.

She must be talking to him on speakerphone. Vanessa doesn't even think for a second to tell Casey that she can hear them. She needs every advantage she can get and if some light reconnaissance is what she needs to do, then so be it. In fact, she quiets her breathing at the risk of sending any sound through the intercom the other direction. Instead, she casually takes a sip from her flute of champagne and glances out the side window.

"Look, Dex, the kids have been saying this portmanteau you find so amusing since . . . well, ever since I was a kid so try to make it sound natural unless you want to become a meme again."

"You're going to have to explain 'portmanteau' to me, too."

"Very funny. So, do you want to stay with us tonight? There's a crew yurt right next to Jeremy's for Mike and me!"

"No, thanks. I'm Dex Derickson, not fucking Bear Grylls."

The car whisks through a shaded glen, ferns blurring past the rear side windows. She wonders which of these cars Dex is sitting in, or drinking in, as the case may be. So far, their conversation hasn't proved to be too revealing. If they keep telling dumb jokes to each other—and especially if Dex refers to himself in the third person again—maybe Vanessa really will tell Casey the intercom is on just to shut them up.

"So, Case, do we have an ending?" Dex's voice comes back.

OK.

This is what Vanessa wants to hear.

The state of play has been murky since Brittani, Zoey, and Becca went home. Vanessa knows she's Jeremy's number one, of course, but she doesn't like the way he's been looking at the other girls lately, and it'd be nice to know who she'll have to beat in the finale.

"I thought talent had more important things to worry about, Mr. Derickson," Casey wisecracks, and Vanessa can see the corner of the producer's satisfied smirk through the partition. "Don't you worry your pretty little head about an ending."

"Call it morbid curiosity, then," Dex responds, his voice staticky, filtered first through the cell phone, then through the intercom, but still discernible. "Who is our illustrious Mr. Blackstone going to pick?"

"Permission to speak freely, sir, Mr. Derickson, sir?" Casey asks, in a mockingly militaristic staccato.

"Let me have it, soldier."

"OK, so Jeremy probably isn't going to pick Lilah-Mae because he actually wants to get his dick wet . . ."

Vanessa has to prevent herself from audibly saying, "Damn." It's a good burn, and it's refreshing to know that Lilah-Mae's just as much of a joke to production as she is to her.

Casey looks through the partition using her rearview mirror, briefly making eye contact with Vanessa before she turns away, maybe a little too abruptly. She reaches for the bottle of champagne in the ice bucket on the floor, carefully refilling her flute at an angle so it doesn't make a sound. She has to act casual.

Did Casey notice?

"On his Day Date with Lilah-Mae today," Casey continues, "he apparently fed her some bullshit about faith really mattering for him. But we think he's doing some image rehab. Maybe he wants to run for office. Either that or he knows Lilah-Mae's family is super rich, which means, despite everything, she's still on the table . . ."—Casey pauses to catch her breath—". . . We know he doesn't want Renee because, well, how can I put this . . ."

"I get it," Dex tells Casey. "Just get him to keep her this week. We want her to break the precedent, right? Make Network happy. Let them have their progressive talking point, even if it means messing with our process. Put someone else on the chopping block if you have to."

For weeks now, she has been trying to figure out why Jeremy hasn't sent Renee home. But the minor satisfaction of solving that mystery is immediately washed away by the anxiety of realizing there is only one open slot left in the finale. If Renee's a lock no matter what, that means Vanessa is competing directly against Lilah-Mae and Amanda for the sole remaining spot. This week just became a three-person melee.

"We've already got the Renee situation under control," Casey says. "I had a little chat with Jeremy on the plane—and then he spoke with her on the ferry. But Dex, are you really trying to *work* right now?"

"I have to earn that executive producer credit somehow," Dex says. "So, who's our final girl: strawberry blonde or platinum blonde? Andrea or Vixen?"

Seems like he didn't spend any time after the ferry ride memorizing their names.

"Amanda or Vanessa," Casey says. "Well, he likes both of them. We caught him and Amanda half-naked in the bathroom of that yacht we filmed in back in Newport."

WHAT?!

Vanessa noticed that he had gone to the bathroom for a long time, but *that's* what he was doing? He must like Amanda more than she thought he did. Is she . . . the frontrunner?

"What? And you didn't tell me about it?" Dex says.

"I mean, not to be crass about it, Dex," Casey responds, "but we would have notified you if Jeremy had made it all the way, um, inside. Then we'd have problems. But we handled it, yelled at them, reminded them of their contracts, and Jeremy's been a good boy ever since. Besides, I didn't want to wake you."

"And Vanessa?"

Vanessa perks up, then catches herself.

Casey pauses and for a moment glances through the rearview mirror to the backseat. Vanessa looks out the window, trying to remain collected, peering at the meadow blurring past, watching white wildflowers trace little lines in the whoosh of greenery.

Casey says the next part quieter: "I think he *knows* he can fuck her whenever he wants. Amanda has put up a little more of a chase, mostly because I'm not sure she even realizes she's on a show about him, but if Vanessa wants to win, she's going to have to step it up tonight. Amanda's a legitimate threat to her frontrunner status and Lilah-Mae's still in the mix, too."

Fuck.

"And we're happy with any of them?" Dex asks, his voice crackling at the end.

"I think we're win-win-win: Lilah-Mae would keep the base happy, and if he wants to pick Villainous Vanessa"—Vanessa tries not to scoff at the nickname—"we'll have a controversial ending like we did in season four," Casey continues. "If it's Airhead Amanda in the end, we'll tone down the ditz edit and try to spin it as two entrepreneurs joining forces or something.

Did you know she sells handbags from Malaysia? They have the word *cute* on them, spelled with a *2* instead of a *t*."

"The American dream," Dex deadpans, then lowers his voice an octave. "Thanks for the report, soldier."

"You got it, boss . . . Oh, turn here, Mike!"

"I got it," Mike snaps back at her.

Mike takes a left turn and the car starts climbing Mount Resilience, which looked gentle from a distance but is still—as the pit forming in Vanessa's stomach can attest—a mountain, with huge elevation gains over short spans of road. Thankfully, Mike takes the switchbacks slower than he did the late-night drive to the B&B, even decelerating to let the occasional car merge back onto the road from the turnoffs that branch off toward scenic overlooks. There aren't many tourists—it's shoulder season in a market well past its prime—but they still pass a Subaru every now and again.

Vanessa downs the rest of her champagne. After what she just learned, she needs it. Five minutes ago, she felt like she was being driven to her coronation. Now she's being carted off to a fucking battle royale.

As the car climbs, the sun is just beginning to dip down in the sky. Through a brief break in the trees, Vanessa can see the vast expanse of water surrounding Otters Island, dazzling under the burnt-orange autumn sun. Dotted among the sea are the rest of the tree-covered San Juan Islands, scattered like lily pads across the blue.

And perhaps it's the thinning oxygen, or the buoyancy from half a bottle of bubbly, but as the car continues ascending toward the summit, Vanessa starts to feel icy calm returning to her veins. She's got an inside track now. She's informed. So what if Jeremy got a little fresh with Amanda back in Rhode Island? Boys will be boys, wandering eyes and all. Vanessa will just have to make sure the Catch is locked onto her from now on. And who cares if Renee gets to be a sacrificial lamb in the finale? That just means Vanessa will be able to enjoy Jeremy—in every sense of the word—instead of having to spend next week fighting for him.

"Hey, Case?" Dex's voice comes crackling through the intercom again.

"Yeah, boss?" Casey says into her phone.

"Let's go glamping."

"That's better! Now you're getting the hang of it."

findingkate.blogtropolis.com

HIKE NUMBER EIGHT TODAY. Still no clues or theories. Just a feeling.

The whole trip takes about six hours with stops for lunch, snacks, and water. The trail smells fantastic—all those pine needles baking in the sun—and it's windy, but there are no obvious places where one of them could have strayed, let alone all three of them. The markings and signposts are clear and well-maintained. My sister once lost her bearings in the Sierra Nevadas and still made it to the main trail by nightfall.

The first third of the hike is almost directly adjacent to the lake, save for a few elevated sections—rocky overlooks where you can sit and enjoy a serene view of the water. They could have fallen into the lake maybe, but Kate, Alice, and Marilyn were strong swimmers and besides, how could *all* three of them have fallen in at once? (Not that the authorities ever bothered to dispatch divers.)

No, every time I retrace Kate's steps, I sit here on the top of Mount Resilience to catch my breath and feel confident that they at least made it this far, but maybe only this far. Something doesn't feel right.

The peak is bald—just a base of enormous, eroded boulders at the top with a handful of anemic-looking leafless trees poking out through the cracks between them, like arms worn down to their sinews reaching up to be fed.

The view, though, is completely captivating. Panoramic. It looks like Middle Earth or something. It should feel peaceful to sit up here, but it doesn't.

There's a stone observatory at the top, towering over you like a panopticon in an old prison. And it's the strangest thing: it took me until now to notice it, but there aren't even any birds up here. As you hike along the summit trail, you see plenty of them: big birds of prey—even the occasional bald eagle—circling overhead. Then, when you get to the summit, there's nothing. Nothing but silence and sky. It feels like the end of the world.

What's wrong with this place? How can somewhere so beautiful be so ugly, too? And why do I keep staying up here longer and longer, even when I don't want to?

Maybe it's because part of me feels like I can actually think up here, or *not* think if I don't want to. I can breathe on this mountain. I can watch the sun dip below the horizon and spend an hour contemplating the particular shade of orange that bleeds from the water as it does. All of that nonsense back in the city—everyone rushing around, caffeine-addled and crazy—has no place up here. I feel like I can scratch past the surface of things and dig my hands into the dirt.

Maybe I am getting answers, just not to the questions I asked.

—Abigail Choi 07/01/04

Renee

Renee traces the tongues of the campfire as they try to climb past the tops of the sparse and scraggly pines, forking off and crackling into thin, vanishing tendrils before they can even reach her shoulders.

She feels the heat of the fire on her face as she stands in a neat row with the other girls, the occasional blast of wind blowing smoke into their faces. At an angle off to the side are Dex and Jeremy, standing together. Opposite them, a small posse of camera guys and crew assemble like black-shirted ghosts, waiting to capture the proceedings, the blinking lights of their equipment indistinguishable from the star-dotted sky.

The filmed portion of Date Night is taking place around a fire pit built into the center of the stone expanse atop Mount Resilience, but on the outskirts are six yurts, evenly arrayed around the circumference of the roughly oval clearing, except for two clustered up north, presumably for whichever crew members have been tasked with babysitting Jeremy. Renee still resents him for telling her his plans on the ferry—but in a way it's comforting to know that what happens tonight doesn't matter in the slightest. She could speak only in limericks from here on out and Jeremy would still pick her.

Palm Springs, she reminds herself, mostly to keep from ripping off her lav mic and running down the mountainside before filming begins.

There's no time to abandon ship anyway. Dex steps forward, finds his mark, fiddles with his cuff links, and launches into his rote lines. It's incredible how quickly this man can switch on. One second, he's a middle-aged guy in a suit, the next, he's an almost mythological being: a glossy, plasticine TV host who makes eye contact with cameras more easily than he does with people.

"Ladies, welcome to Date Night," Dex projects, as though he's commentating a football game. "We're here atop historic Mount Resilience for a night of glamping. Each of you will get to spend a night in your own beautiful luxury yurt, courtesy of Salish Shelters."

Dex gestures in a circle toward the yurts, faint white domes emerging from the dark stone of the clearing in the distance. Then the host turns to face the women and Renee stifles the urge to burst out laughing at the ridiculousness of the show's theatrics. All the women look deathly serious. Meanwhile, Dex acts like he's hosting *Legends of the Hidden Temple* or *American Ninja Warrior* or something, and that disjuncture won't ever feel normal, no matter how long this ordeal drags on.

How did Renee end up here, in the farthest corner of the continental United States, camping with three girls who look like they have never had dirt under their fingernails in their lives? Amanda's petite body swims awkwardly in an unbuttoned flannel shirt, Vanessa must be freezing in red denim booty shorts that make her look like she's in an eighties summer camp movie, and Lilah-Mae's outfit—a white blouse and seersucker pants—is one or two accessories away from being suitable for a Sunday service. If she even goes to a church that allows women to wear pants. Renee has chosen to dress more comfortably: jeans, a white undershirt, a flannel that actually fits her.

And then there's Dex, wearing a $5,000 suit on top of a mountain for what will probably end up being five seconds of screen time.

All this pageantry for a show that America believes is about true love. But it's just dress-up, isn't it? They're all wearing costumes. Especially Jeremy, whose metrosexual lumberjack look—a puffy vest, jeans, and boots—isn't that much more flattering on him than that neon atrocity of a tracksuit was.

Dex continues his Date Night speech: "Ladies, Jeremy has some tough decisions to make. Tomorrow morning, at the Elimination Event, two of you will be heading home. It's all on the line tonight. If you've been holding anything back, tonight is when you let it go. Tonight is the night for hard truths to come out. So tonight, you'll be playing Truth or Dare around this very campfire. Good luck."

OK, now this is just getting silly. First, mud wrestling back in Atlanta, and now this?

How old are we?

Renee blinks, stunned, as the other women clap and cheer for the cameras, with a girlish enthusiasm that's either forced or real but annoying either way. They scamper over to the tree stump seats that have been arranged in a circle around the campfire, but Renee remains motionless as the crew swims past and around her like a school of fish.

She sees Dex take off his lav, pull it out through his already-unbuttoned dress shirt, and hand it to Casey. Renee enjoys spying on moments like this because it reminds her that this is all just make-believe. That the legendary Dex Derickson is just some guy. "What makes this mountain 'historic,' Casey? That it's old, like *all* mountains?" Renee overhears Dex complain, as he loosens his tie. "And that last cue card had the word 'tonight' on it *four sentences* in a row. Honestly, we need better writers. It's getting embarrassing."

"I'll get right on that, boss," Casey says. "Are you good to take a car back down to the hotel yourself? It's just going to be Mike and me up here overnight, but the other crew won't be heading down until after Truth or Dare. So unless you want to stay for the game . . ."

"As riveting as that sounds, Casey, I'll take a car down now. I've got a Date Night of my own with some shellfish."

"Careful," Casey says. "Don't catch crabs."

Renee groans at the joke but they can't hear her.

"That was bad," Dex tells her, "even for you."

And as Dex heads off toward the small parking lot at the south end of the clearing, Renee wishes she could leave with him instead of reliving a middle school rite of passage. Is any hotel really worth the humiliation of playing Truth or Dare as an adult? Maybe not. But a tap on the shoulder jolts her back to reality.

"Care to join us, Ren?"

Ugh.

At this point she should start calling him "Jer" and see how he likes it. She turns to find the Catch smiling at her, the grease from his pomade creating a weird shiny glint on his forehead just below his hairline. This is a man best looked at from a distance of fifteen to twenty feet—or better yet, not at all.

Behind him, the girls have already plopped their butts down on the tree stumps. The cameramen are settling into their initial positions, except for Mike, who apparently followed Jeremy with a handheld to capture this candid moment.

"Sure, Jeremy," Renee says, following him over to the fireside. She takes the sole remaining open stump between Lilah-Mae and Vanessa.

"OK, girls," Jeremy says, setting himself down on his preappointed seat.

He glances over at Casey, who is hovering just around the edge of the fire, to ensure he has the all clear before continuing: "As Dex said, I've got some tough decisions to make before tomorrow's Elimination Event, so let's be honest with each other. But most importantly, let's have some fun. I'll start."

Cameramen swirl around the circle like spirits in the night, already searching for every reaction, every look, no matter how subtle.

"Renee, truth or dare?" Jeremy asks her.

Renee blinks at him from across the fire. The firelight makes the greasy sheen on his forehead glisten even brighter. She imagines sharing any true feeling she has about Jeremy—or about anyone on *The Catch* for that matter—and asks for a dare.

"Starting with a dare—I like it!" Jeremy says, clapping his hands and rubbing them together. "Hmm, let's see: I dare you to tell the truth about how you feel about me."

Come on.

"Isn't that cheating?" Lilah-Mae asks. "She asked for a dare, not truth."

Renee is fuming inside. It was one thing for Jeremy to let her know in advance he wasn't going to pick her. She was fine giving the producers inauthentic pat responses during her ITMs; she's been lying to them for weeks already. But to put her on the spot in front of everyone? To ask her for public validation when he's already told her she's not the one? This just feels like twisting the knife.

"Well, Jeremy," Renee says, looking across the fire at the Catch and choosing her words carefully, "I have very strong feelings about you, and if you want to know more, you'll just have to speak with me privately."

"Ooh!" Amanda says, like they're all at a sleepover and Renee just admitted she liked a boy.

"OK, I'm taking over," Vanessa declares, turning to Jeremy. "Because this is a pretty boring game of Truth or Dare so far. No offense, babe."

Renee is still angry, the fire almost seeming to flare up in sync with the little grunt she permits herself. A camera probably caught her. She doesn't care. They'll be able to edit her having any sort of reaction they want her to have anyway. The slightest sigh can be taken and shown out of context to make her seem shockingly bitchy and rude. Jeremy acquiesces to Vanessa, who scoots forward to the edge of her tree stump.

"Amanda," Vanessa announces to the group, "I dare you to kiss anyone around this fire who's *not* Jeremy."

Renee's heart drops to her stomach. She watches Lilah-Mae on the stump to her right cast a glance behind them, trying to see if anyone is going to intervene but of course they won't. The *Catch* producers live for uncomfortable situations like these. She wouldn't be shocked if Casey had been the one to suggest the idea to Vanessa.

"Well," Amanda says, rising from her stump and surveying the women around the fire, "of course, I'd *rather* kiss Jeremy, but if I had to choose . . ."

"Can I take myself out of the running?" Lilah-Mae asks, raising her hand.

Vanessa is ready to pounce, almost standing up in her seat. "Oh? *Why*, Lilah-Mae?"

When Vanessa finds a button that irritates Lilah-Mae, she presses it over and over again until it breaks.

"You know exactly why, Vanessa," Lilah-Mae whips back. "I have nothing against Amanda doing the dare if she wants to, but I don't want to participate."

"Bold of you to assume she would pick you, L.M.," says Vanessa. "You must think you're pretty hot."

"Girls," Jeremy intervenes, too late for his words to mean anything. "Let's let Amanda decide."

Renee spots Lilah-Mae shooting the Catch a look of betrayal, as if she expected him to put a stop to the dare altogether after the producers tacitly refused to intervene.

Meanwhile, Amanda taps her pouting lips, looking back and forth between Vanessa and Renee. Renee regards the girl from across the fire and notices the way the strawberry undertones in her loose, messy curls seem to absorb the warmth of the flickering light. Her button nose wrinkles in concentration, as she makes eye contact first with Renee, then with Vanessa, before fixing her gaze on Renee again. As Amanda nibbles one side of her lower lip, Renee feels warm waves of desire lapping up from her feet, rising through her body, and threatening to burst out of her breast.

Is Amanda's head as pretty and empty as a Fabergé egg? Yes. Does every conversation of theirs turn into Amanda asking Renee why she isn't on Glamstapix? Yes. Does Renee want Amanda to kiss her? Also, yes.

God, yes.

The wavering effect emanating from the firelight only adds to the dreamlike quality of Amanda walking over to Renee, who stares back at the girl, transfixed.

"Renee, do you mind?" Amanda asks.

Renee can only shake her head.

Amanda leans over, her artfully disheveled hair falling like a halo around Renee's face, and even though they are surrounded by cameras and crew, it feels like they are alone on this mountaintop. Renee locks eyes with Amanda, who smiles, and shuts her own.

And then Renee feels the other woman's lips pressing against hers, urgent but not insistent, hungry but not desperate. Renee kisses her back, delicately at first, but then, unable to control herself, she reaches out her tongue to feel Amanda's lips, which taste sweet like chocolate and champagne. But Amanda has already pulled away, seemingly oblivious to the significance of this perfect moment.

Renee looks up to find Amanda turned to the others, her arms raised in mock triumph.

"Whoo! When on Otters Island, right?" Amanda says. "My gay moms would be so proud!"

She cackles, with Vanessa and Jeremy following in suit. Three hyenas laughing in the night. This is a joke to them. Something in Renee had finally unlocked. Something beautiful and secret and, most important, *hers*—and they are *laughing*. Vanessa even gives Amanda a high five for executing the dare before she sits back down as Jeremy lets loose a long, satisfied exhale.

"Whew!"

Renee tries to ensure no cameras are monitoring her facial expressions, but of course they are. Their lenses glare and glow like the eyeshine of predators lurking in the shadows.

"Is it my turn yet?" Lilah-Mae asks, her stern tone cutting through the others' laughter.

"Oh, did that make you uncomfortable, L.M.?" Vanessa taunts. "Or maybe it turned you on? Do you need to go repent?"

To these girls—to Jeremy, and perhaps especially to Casey—Renee is just a pawn on the board. A pawn they're more than willing to sacrifice to get the positioning they want.

"What's your problem, Vanessa?" Lilah-Mae yells. "Why can't you just play the game?"

"You want to play Truth or Dare?" Vanessa fires back. "Because I've got a question for you!"

Renee hears the blood throbbing in her eardrums and feels like she is leaving her body, like she is becoming one of the nameless viewers watching this scene from a distance, both temporal and physical. As the other voices escalate around her, Renee realizes that none of this means anything. She knew that it was silly before, but now she feels the inconsequentiality of it deeply, at a bone level. It's all just white noise, building to a dull roar that grows in volume until Renee can swear it's coming from the trees.

But the girls are shouting over it.

"Oh yeah?!" Lilah-Mae asks. "What's your question, Vanessa?"

Vanessa's face goes steely, the red tones of the firelight flickering on her skin.

"Here's my question," she hisses at Lilah-Mae. "When were you planning on telling the world you worked at Hooters your entire time at Baylor?"

"What?!" Lilah-Mae screeches, just quickly enough to be telling.

"Don't play dumb, L.M. I was doing an auto show in Dallas after the *Catch* cast was announced and met some former friends of yours." Vanessa folds her arms in triumph. "So the Hooters girl becomes a Christian pageant queen to get more Glamstapix followers? Why not be open about that? Why hide it from everyone?"

"You're dressed like you work at Hooters right now!" Lilah-Mae screams.

"But I don't. Because I'm actually hot enough to model, not just do pageants."

"Yeah, model with *cars*."

The cameras press in close, drawn in by the drama like planets drifting toward a collapsing star. Renee barely emerges from her dissociative state long enough to turn around and spot Casey at the edge of the firelight, her body outlined by one of the yurts in the distance, an enormous Cheshire grin spread across her face. Jeremy is sitting there, dumbly, mouth agape. These people are sick. All of them, sick. Renee would kill to see what they'll look like when they're fifty and all their fillers have worn off, their faces turning into drooping Dalí paintings faster than they can keep injecting fat into them.

"That decision was between me and the Lord, Vanessa!" Lilah-Mae shouts. "My sins were scarlet, and He made them white as wool. Meanwhile, you had an abortion *six months ago*."

Everything falls quiet. Even a couple of crew guys drop equipment.

Lilah-Mae lets out one final burst: "That's right. I'm not the only one whose friends have loose lips."

Renee feels like she's watching a stage play, like she's in a movie or a book. It's not that this doesn't feel real; it's that it feels *too* real, *too* heightened.

Vanessa's voice when she speaks has a quality Renee has never heard in it before: raw, wounded, on the brink of sobs.

"Fuck you, Lilah-Mae," she says. "Fuck you."

"I'm going to bed," Lilah-Mae announces, rising from her stump. "I guess we'll see who's still here tomorrow."

At this point, it would be fine with Renee if none of them were.

findingkate.blogtropolis.com

I SAW SOMETHING at the peak today.

At least, I think I saw something.

It could explain everything. I'm scared and yet I want to see it again—can't think about anything *but* seeing it again. My in-town espionage feels stale now. Irrelevant. Who cares about the islanders?

If what I saw is real, the truth could be so simple—and so extraordinary.

I don't want to write more until I'm sure.

Let's just say I've decided to become a nature photographer after all.

—Abigail Choi, 07/20/04

Amanda

T he inside of this yurt is so freaking cute. Like, seriously adorable.

Amanda wishes she could hop on Glamstapix Live and give her followers a video tour, or even just shoot a quick Glimmer panorama of the space to set to music. After that toxic game of Truth or Dare, she could use the warmth and positivity of her fans right about now. Their red heart emojis would fill up her phone screen and she could just bask in their ruby glow, forgetting all about the shouting match between V and Lilah-Mae.

If only she had her phone. But she can at least record a video to post later. Spare moments are often the best for making sponsored content. Her desk-job friends back in LA get to switch off when they punch out; Amanda doesn't have that luxury. Time is money, which means wasted time is essentially an operating expense.

She pulls the point-and-shoot camera out of the pocket of her flannel, switches it to video mode, points it at a blank stretch of the yurt's canvas, and hits "record." After a brief vocal warmup—"red leather, yellow leather"—she begins.

"Oh my God, you guys, I just wanted to give you a behind-the-scenes look at those to-die-for yurts from week nine," she narrates, sweeping the camera up to the ceiling, where approximately three-dozen wooden posts converge to hold up the tent's crown.

"I love this pink Turkish lamp dangling from the center of the yurt—it's exactly the sort of luxurious touch you would never expect when you go camping."

She pans the camera down to the bamboo floor next.

"And this ocher rug? I think it's Turkish, too. I love how the geometric pattern is modern, but still has these super distinctive classic touches."

She points the camera at the small white appliance sitting on the chest at the foot of the bed.

"Do you hear that peaceful sound, you guys? Like there's a gentle river outside? That's coming from this white-noise machine, which makes each of the yurts feel like its own little world. I'll have to look up the company that makes these, because you guys know I *need* one back home at my place in WeHo."

Another sponsorship opportunity, maybe.

Amanda lifts the camera up to eye-level so it can capture the pièce de résistance: the four-poster king bed in all its glory, shrouded in some kind of decorative white mosquito netting.

"This lace canopy around the bed is such a smart design: not only does it look super cute—like a bridal veil, almost—it should keep flying critters out. You guys all know that bug bites turn into golf balls on my legs, and I want to wear my green Kitri tea dress to the Elimination tomorrow. And just a reminder, you guys, you can always use my code APARKS10 when you buy direct from Kitri for ten percent off!"

She walks around the bed, careful to keep the camera steady as she does. She wouldn't want to make any of her fans as motion sick as Lilah-Mae apparently got on her helicopter date. *Yuck.* If Jeremy doesn't send her home after she almost yakked on him, she doesn't know what it's going to take.

"I love this fireplace—and I saw a chimney outside so I think it is actually a real wood-burning fireplace," Amanda continues, nudging the camera to the right now. "And this small vanity is perfect. It beats getting ready with a compact mirror, which is what I usually have to do when I go camping."

Amanda hasn't gone camping since her Girl Scout days. But it's not quite lying: at camp one time, she did use a compact she had stolen from her femmier mom.

Amanda swivels around 180 degrees to see if she's missed anything else she wants to show her fans before spouting off her second and final ad. Nope. The other side of the yurt is blank canvas.

"And that's about it, guys! The only thing on that side of the yurt is the 'door,' which, well, it's not much of a door, is it?"

Amanda zooms in on the six-foot-long zipper in the canvas that hooks onto an interior latch at the top of the slit. Time to wave goodbye. It's hard to put yourself in frame without a front-facing camera, but if Paris Hilton and Britney Spears could do it back in 2006, so can Amanda. She manages to flip the point-and-shoot around for the end of the video.

"I know by the time you see this, we'll all know how *The Catch* ended, but I just want to say that even while I've been away from you guys, I've felt your love, your warmth, and your positivity, and it's made all the difference for me. Thank you for that, and please know, I love you guys, too. Mwah!"

From her pants pocket, Amanda produces the small spray bottle she's been saving for this moment. "I'm headed off to dreamland now, you guys. I know a lot of people only put on perfume at the start of the day or before they go somewhere, but I always like to spritz myself with this rose-water mist right before I fall sleep. It helps center and soothe me—and plus I wake up smelling *ah*-mazing. I'll drop the link to this along with a discount code in the comments below!"

She performatively sprays the rose water into the air with a flourish, lets the mist settle around her, then slips the bottle back into the pocket of her jeans. The scent of it is actually kind of acrid and artificial, but she gets a good rate on click-throughs.

"OK, byeeeeeeeeeee!" she squeals, with a blown kiss at the lens. *And scene.*

Now that she's done recording, Amanda can finally sneeze. The rose-water mist *always* makes her sneeze. But at last she can relax. There are no producers anymore, no cameras clanging around, just a light wind batting against the canvas and the gentle sound of coursing water coming from the white-noise machine. The yurts are all spread far apart across the mountaintop—so that they can get a dramatic drone shot in the morning—and Amanda feels grateful now for the extra space.

She pulls back the veil around the bed, tying it out of the way with the silk sash she finds draped across the pillows. It really is a cute yurt. She wasn't just saying that for Glamstapix. She removes the red-and-black flannel shirt she has never worn before in her life, peels off her Patagonia tank top, and unzips her jeans, tugging them down to the floor. This is the first night since filming began that she has had her own room and she is living for it.

Leaping back onto the bed in her underwear, Amanda is free. Glamping tonight feels like a reward for every post, every hard-earned follower—even the ones she paid for—and every dollar she has made from handbag sales. In this business, "making it" always feels elusive and far away, always sliding just out of reach the second you're on the cusp of it, but she's finally close now. Maybe she can draw a salary from her handbag sales after this, instead of pouring all the money right back into internet marketing.

Goosebumps form on Amanda's skin as the cold of the night seeps in. The yurt might be cute, but without wood burning in the fireplace, it's essentially a refrigerator.

She scoots off the edge of the bed and extracts a pajama romper from her suitcase that she wouldn't mind a man seeing her in. After eight weeks of Jeremy trying to sneak into her hotel room—and especially after they came *so* close in Newport—Amanda knows better than to dismiss the possibility of late-night interruptions. It's a cute, tartan-print piece that she likes to wear on Christmas Eve, and it feels appropriately celebratory. She's finishing the second-to-last button when she hears the shuffling of footsteps outside the doorway.

That was fast.

Though Amanda wonders how Jeremy could have escaped Casey's watchful eye so soon. His yurt was set up right next to hers and Mike's for a reason. After Casey caught them on that yacht, she started keeping the Catch on a shorter leash. But it doesn't matter how he got away: if this is Amanda's chance to cement her win, she'll take it.

Jeremy isn't bad. Kind of skeezy, but she's slept with worse. And none of those music festival guys came with an opportunity to quadruple her Glamstapix following overnight. The only things they left Amanda with were pubes in the shower and used condoms draped over those tiny hotel bathroom waste bins. Eww. What was that slogan she learned as a Brownie? *Pack it in, pack it out?*

There's a scratching on the outside of the canvas door, which is odd, but it's impossible to really knock on a yurt, isn't it?

"Hang on, Jeremy, I think I have to unhook the zipper from the inside!" she calls out toward the entryway.

She wishes Jeremy had better style, at least. On the rare days when his outfits aren't provided by the show, he wears Lacoste polos and boardshorts. She'll have to pick out his clothes for him after the finale airs, at least when they're doing on-camera press together. Off camera, he can wear that heinous tracksuit as much as he wants. Then after a month or two, when she announces the end of their relationship in a long and heartfelt Glamstapix caption, Jeremy can go right back to looking like he's about to beat up nerds in the year 2003.

As Amanda wraps up some last-minute tidying, shoving her dirty clothes under the bed and disguising the messiness of her hair with a ponytail, she hears Jeremy tugging at the zipper across the yurt. The canvas around the door jostles with each of his frantic attempts. Maybe he didn't hear her.

"OK, eager beaver!" Amanda yells. "I'm coming!"

Well, probably not.

That's why Amanda packed her Rabbit. She was surprised production didn't confiscate it along with her smartphone—but it makes sense. You can't get the internet on a vibrator . . . yet.

She reaches out to unhook the zipper at the top but before she can grasp it, it rips all the way down to the floor, seemingly of its own volition in one swift, sudden motion, the latch coming loose and flying across the yurt.

"Jeremy! Don't break it!"

Cold air rushes in through the slit. Amanda leans forward to open the canvas flap so that Jeremy can come in before the temperature drops even more. But as she nears the threshold, she hears breathing. It's heavier than Jeremy's. More primal. She takes a step back.

A head bursts through the canvas, covered in shaggy, sweat-caked hair. Amanda screams. But even as she trips over the Turkish rug, tumbling ass-first onto the floor, she can't help but take in every feature of the thing's twisted face: its flaring nostrils sniffing ravenously at the air, glowing yellow eyes, and pouting lips.

That's not Jeremy.

At first, Amanda registers it as a dog or a bear, but it looks almost human, its contours twisting into an expression that is equal parts hunger and despair—a deep, almost prehistoric longing. Some kind of monkey? On Otters Island? Amanda yells at the animal.

"Get away!"

But the long oval face simply casts its amber eyes down on her, craning its neck slowly and purposefully. Drool drips off its thin lips onto the yurt's bamboo floor. It sniffs at the air again. Her rose-water spray? Is that what it's smelling? Amanda screams again, hoping that one of the others—Casey, Jeremy, anyone—can hear her from across the clearing, but the thing opens its mouth, too, and lets loose a deafening yawp that rattles the joists holding up the tent.

Oh fuck, oh fuck, oh fuck.

Amanda shuffles backward, crab-walking toward the king bed, but the ape from hell plods straight through the canvas slit, its body hunched over but still held upright by two muscular legs blanketed with thick, shaggy hair. Heaving from the force of its own breath, it finally comes into full view under the pink-hued lamp.

Staring up at it, frozen with shock, Amanda spots two breasts poking out of its hair-covered torso with a perkiness that for a fleeting moment reminds her of the nude Jean Paul Gaultier cone bra from Madonna's Blond Ambition tour—a random thought that flees from her mind as she realizes this thing is easily strong enough to maim her.

The hulking beast straightens up. It must be at least seven, eight feet tall now, with arms hanging almost to its knees. A lady ape? That walks on two legs? Is this some kind of fucking nightmare? Is she *still* on that bad Coachella trip? But the musty, dog-like stench flooding Amanda's nasal cavity is all too real. The thing reeks.

"Casey! V!" she tries them all in succession from the floor. "Renee! Lilah-Mae! MIIIKE!"

Why hasn't anyone come yet? The damn noise machines?

The only sound she hears above the artificial roar of water is *it*. This monstrous thing, with its furry feet planted firmly on the bamboo floor, and its breasts rising and falling faster as it pants. Pressing her back up against the foot of the bed, Amanda stands on shaking legs that feel like twigs compared to the creature's stocky limbs.

The ape regards her with a keen intelligence, seeming to size Amanda up just as carefully as Amanda does her. Its shoulders move up and down with each grunting breath. The animal is strong, yes, but hopefully it is slow.

Amanda sees the thing take a half-step forward and she can sense that this is her chance to get out. Maybe her only one before it gets too close. She launches herself toward the door of the yurt, trying to skirt around the creature, fighting every instinct that tells her to run in the opposite direction.

As she rushes forward to the left side of the she-ape, Amanda almost faints from the overpowering smell of the thing, mildewy and strong, but what she sees in the corner of her vision shoots adrenaline into her veins: the thing is swiveling its head to watch her run, its thin lips curled upward into something resembling a grin. But it is too late to go back now.

She leaps toward the opening in the yurt's canvas, gulping down cold air as it hits her face. It tastes like freedom—like life. For a second, Amanda almost wishes there were cameras around to capture what must be a perfect freeze frame of her leaping into the black night.

And then Amanda realizes she is stuck in midair, the hair on the back of her head pulled taut as the monkey grabs hold of her ponytail. Pain shoots through her scalp as she is yanked backward with a wrenching force, back through the slit in the canvas, back toward the overpowering smell of wet fur, back into the yurt where no one heard her cries. The last thing she sees before her head slams hard against the bamboo floor is the shaggy creature from below, toe to head. It seems to stretch up forever, like one of the trees listening silently to her screams.

Vanessa

Vanessa knows she's not dreaming because why would Renee be in her dreams? The girl is about as memorable as a block of cement. So why the hell is she walking into her yurt at . . . one in the morning? Yes, through bleary eyes, Vanessa confirms the time on the old-fashioned gold-plated alarm clock sitting on her nightstand.

"Renee?" she asks, clearing a frog in her throat.

Vanessa groggily watches Renee fiddle with the flap door of the tent, which she somehow managed to open from the outside, although it looks like she may have broken it in the process.

"Amanda is missing," the other girl says, turning around and stopping just inside the tent opening, her voice flat, dispassionate.

It takes Vanessa a few dazed seconds to process the information.

"Did you check the bathroom?"

She shudders at the thought of the wooden outhouse she had braved before bed: a gaping hole in the ground that could extend for miles below for all she could tell. If she has to pee again before they return to civilization, she'll just squat behind a tree.

Vanessa sits up in bed, stretches, and looks at Renee, whose hair is tied up under a scarf, her big brown eyes oddly calm. Renee doesn't look all that concerned about Amanda's being gone. She's acting dutiful, almost obligated to share the news.

"Casey checked the outhouse. And Lilah-Mae thinks she heard some kind of noise from over by Amanda's yurt. Like, maybe an animal."

The only good thing about the outhouse, Vanessa remembers, is that it was closest to Lilah-Mae's yurt, which means she's the one who had to smell it all night long. She deserves to be dunked in it for saying what she did on camera at Date Night, the fucking bitch. L.M. couldn't have picked a more damaging secret to air in front of America. Abortions, Vanessa has found, are a lot like affairs: lots of women have them and lots of women judge you for having them, and often those two groups of women are the same.

Let Lilah-Mae tell herself she wouldn't have made the same choice.

Vanessa never told anyone about her abortion—except for a fellow model after an exhausting show in Salt Lake when they got drinks together at the hotel bar. Vanessa thought they'd never see each other again. They barely knew each other's first names. But that girl must have told someone else, who told someone else—and then word must have spread around Glamstapix circles until it landed on Lilah-Mae's ears.

Fuck her.

"L.M. thinks she heard an animal?" Vanessa asks Renee. "I mean, she also thinks two of every animal took a cruise together, so . . ."

Renee laughs for a second, but catches herself, "Yeah, I think Lilah-Mae might be right about this one though. Casey and Mike even called the cops. They should be here soon."

Vanessa hears distant commotion outside the unzipped yurt door. Footsteps. Voices. She sits up with a jerk, feels the chill air that Renee let into the tent with her, and gathers the sheets around herself. *Is this serious?*

"Wait, really?" Vanessa asks her, swinging her feet around onto the bamboo floor.

"Yeah."

Vanessa knows the chances of Amanda getting attacked by an animal in the middle of the night are one in a million. But still, it'd be annoying if she wandered off somewhere and hurt herself. It could delay production by a day or two. Amanda would get a cast over her broken leg, which she would hate because she wouldn't be able to wear any of her tighter outfits over it. Worse still, Jeremy would probably feel pressure to give her a corsage out of pity at the Elimination Event—and thanks to Casey's intercom slip, it's clear now that there's only one finale spot left. Is this Amanda's way of angling for it? Is she actually a secret genius?

"How's Jeremy holding up?" Vanessa asks.

Renee visibly recoils at the question, glancing past her to stare at the fireplace and shake her head. Vanessa thinks she even hears a little "tsk" escape Renee's lips.

"*He's* who you're worried about right now?"

"What? Am I not allowed to be concerned about my future fiancé?" Vanessa pulls on the coat that she hung over her bedpost before she passed out. She hadn't been able to get under the covers fast enough after filming Date Night in her short shorts. She wore them so that Jeremy could see what he has in store for him once he stops lollygagging and picks her already. Not that Jeremy had much time to see how much nicer her ass is than Amanda's, thanks to Lilah-Mae's outburst.

The *Catch* audience deserves to hear about L.M.'s stint at Hooters because the girl is clearly pretending to be something she's not while simultaneously judging everyone around her. It's about the hypocrisy of it all.

Vanessa has never pretended to be someone else; some parts of her past are just private is all. Private, that is, until a certain Christian beauty queen sticks her redone nose where it doesn't belong. Amanda's gone? Well, Little Miss Dallas–Fort Worth can disappear next for all Vanessa cares. She'd feed Lilah-Mae to a bear in a heartbeat.

"So . . ." Renee says, ignoring Vanessa's question. "Now you know."

The other girl turns away to face the opening in the canvas. Vanessa watches her step toward it, then pause as though she's about to say something.

But Renee just casts her eyes down at the floor and steps out through the slit, leaving Vanessa alone in the yurt.

A moment later, she hears Renee shout toward the center of the clearing: "She's up!"

What the fuck is Renee's problem? She's not a serious threat—eavesdropping on Casey made that much clear—but between yesterday and today, Renee has gotten snippy with Lilah-Mae and now she's being cagey with her. Is she trying to get back in the game? Does she want to make some kind of Hail Mary move on her man, just like this late-season ploy of Amanda's? After a half hour of hiding in the woods, Amanda's going to come back and act so scared that Jeremy will have to comfort her—Vanessa is sure of it.

These conniving little bitches.

Vanessa stands up with fire in her feet. Clearly, she has to get this situation back under control.

She bursts out of the tent and spots the others—all but Casey—in the distance, gathered around the fire pit in the center of the clearing, lit by the last of the glowing embers. Mike looks like he's igniting some kindling beneath the logs to get the flames going in earnest again. Jeremy's standing nearby, too.

Figures.

All guys are entranced by fire.

Lilah-Mae glares from across the fire pit as Vanessa approaches, sidling up to the Catch and placing a reassuring hand on the back of his North Face vest.

"Hey, baby, you doing OK?"

Jeremy looks confused if a tad shaken.

"What? Yeah. I'm OK. I just, uh, hope they find her."

"Do you know what happened?" she asks him, craning her neck up to stare at his chiseled jaw. God, he's tall. And he looks good in his little outdoorsy getup, too. But just when Vanessa is fantasizing about Jeremy picking her up and splitting her in two like a piece of firewood, Lilah-Mae dares speak to her.

"I heard something," she says. "I stayed up after Date Night to do my Bible study and I heard this noise, but it didn't sound . . . human. Then I heard a yell. That's when I went and got Casey and Mike."

Vanessa has half a mind to drag Lilah-Mae into the fire and see what kind of kindling she'd make. She had asked her boyfriend, not the Slut Shamer in Chief, about Amanda's absence. What Lilah-Mae did was unforgivable—the equivalent of siccing an army of attack dogs on her. Vanessa will defend her decisions to the death, but she doesn't want to *literally* die from anthrax poisoning.

"The cameras aren't rolling anymore, Miss Lilah-Mae. You don't need to reassure everyone that you're still a good little Christian girl who reads the Bible every night."

"Our friend is gone, maybe hurt, and you're mad at me for *casually* mentioning that I was reading my Bible?"

Lilah-Mae gives Vanessa an innocent look, but her eyes sparkle mischievously. She knows exactly what she's doing. She always does.

"Whoa, whoa, whoa," Mike intervenes, standing up now that he has successfully brought the fire back to life. "Don't jump to any conclusions. Casey is off calling the police again now for an update on their ETA. We're going to find Amanda. Then we can all go back to bed."

Vanessa looks at Jeremy again. He's staring into the resurrected fire as it inhales oxygen, flames illuminating his face from below. She's never seen him this late at night before, when he has a light dusting of beard shadow. It looks good on him. Maybe he should grow it out. Lean into this whole mountain man aesthetic.

"Vanessa, do you remember when you tried to tell me about that shadow in Amanda's picture?" Lilah-Mae asks.

The gall on this girl.

"Oh, you want to talk about Amanda's picture?" Vanessa's yelling now. "What happened to you thinking we were just trying to get into your head before your 'special day' with Jeremy? As if I'm *at all* threatened by *you*! Never fucking speak to me again."

There's a silence. The fire, almost sensing the break in their argument, crackles and snaps more vigorously. Feet shuffle awkwardly around the pit. Renee idly kicks at the ground. And then Vanessa realizes there's at least one bad thing about Amanda being gone: She has no friends left in this crowd. Certainly not among the girls. Renee is getting bitchier by the minute. Lilah-Mae would probably perform an exorcism on her if she could tie her to a bed—which, let her try.

At least she still has Jeremy.

Vanessa threads her arm through his and snuggles up close to him. "I'm cold."

"Mike, mind if I put another log on this fire?" Jeremy asks, breaking Vanessa's grasp and heading off toward the small wood-pile stacked a few yards away.

What's gotten into him?

Jeremy is usually so attentive. Was Casey right? Could Amanda actually be his first choice? Is that why he's *this* shaken up by her disappearance? Vanessa wouldn't wish death on anyone—even Lilah-Mae, if she's being honest—but if a wolf ate Amanda's leg or something, she would *have* to go home, wouldn't she, and then they could still film the rest of the season? Is that what they all think happened? Some kind of animal attack? No one else suspects a pity play—*really*?

"OK, what the *fuck* is going on?" Vanessa yells, and she's only referring in part to the Amanda situation. She has a lot of questions: Why is Renee being so weird? Why is Jeremy acting distant? What exactly does Lilah-Mae think she heard? Maybe she is dreaming after all because none of them are making any fucking sense.

"I've been trying to tell you," Lilah-Mae says. "I think something took her. That sound . . ."

Casey appears at the fireside, panting from the walk over, her smartphone clenched tight in her hand. Vanessa watches as Mike shoots her a quizzical look, but Casey ignores him.

"Ladies, let's stay calm," the producer says, shoving her phone into the pocket of her windbreaker. "The, uh, park rangers should be here in about thirty minutes."

Jeremy returns with a log, stacks it on the fire, and says nothing. He doesn't return to Vanessa's side, deliberately standing opposite the pit from her.

"Well, in the meantime," Lilah-Mae says, "would anyone mind if I said a quick prayer for Amanda?"

Vanessa parts her lips to let out an exasperated groan but finds that the sound coming out of her mouth is louder than she expected, a booming metallic crunch that, in fact, is not coming from her mouth at all. From somewhere out there in the night comes a crashing noise so loud it must have woken up half the people on this damn island. And in its wake an awful silence.

findingkate.blogtropolis.com

EDITOR'S NOTE, 10/30/04: I debated whether or not to post these blog entries according to the instructions Abby gave me before she moved to Otters Island. I stopped hearing from her on the first of October, so I was technically supposed to start publishing her "findings," as she once called them, earlier this month.

But if my final messages from Abby were any indication, I believe her grip on sanity may have been slipping. It pains me to say that about someone I care about, but it's true. She was growing increasingly erratic, difficult to contact.

Last I heard, she was renting a room in a converted roadside motel in West Bay, handing an envelope of cash to the landlady every month, but it seemed like she was spending most of her nights sleeping on top of Mount Resilience. Her emails were fewer and farther between. Then they stopped for a while.

Her last email to me was only one line long, written at 3 a.m. her time:

"Funny. She has a way of showing you what really matters."

I can say this with confidence: What she thinks she saw up there doesn't exist. I'm no psychologist, but maybe this thing was some sort of projection of her own grief. Perhaps falling back on myth was a way for her to imagine an alternate version of Kate who could have survived in the woods for the past decade. I was hoping that this experience could bring her some closure, even if she was spending all her life savings on a quixotic quest. I thought she would get to Otters Island and realize that the truth is often far more banal than we want it to be: Kate got lost in the woods. The island has no shadowy underworld. Life isn't a B movie. Some people die, and it's just shit luck when you love them before they do. Incompetence is always a better explanation than conspiracy.

Last week, I reached out to the authorities on Otters so that they could perform a wellness check on her. I hope they find her from the alias she used and the physical description I gave them.

In the meantime, I did decide to post these entries after all, mostly to keep my word. I was worried this might encourage people to develop incurable obsessions of their own, but maybe this story can do the opposite: perhaps Abby's journey, however tragic, can show people the importance of leaving the past where it lies so that it doesn't claim them, too.

And Abby, if you're reading this somehow, somewhere, I apologize for blowing your cover, but it's for your own good. Please come home. We miss you.

—REDACTED

[Three]

[Three]

Casey

"What was that?" one of the girls asks.

The second the terrible, gut-rending metallic crunch finishes echoing across the mountaintop, interrupting the still of the night, Casey immediately fears the answer to that question. She fishes her phone out of her windbreaker pocket, sees a missed call notification from Dex time-stamped twenty minutes ago, and flicks her silent switch off.

Fuck.

So he did get her voice mail.

"Sounded like a crash," Mike says, stating the obvious.

Not helping.

Mike should know better than to spook the contestants, but he's been jumpy himself, hasn't he? All of them are huddled around the fire for warmth, waiting for the authorities to come, presumably so they can help disentangle a drunk Amanda from a bush or something—at least that's Casey's current theory about what happened. She checked the champagne bottles in the town cars before Date Night, and it was as she predicted: neither Renee nor Lilah-Mae touched them, but Vanessa and Amanda each drank half of theirs. Casey even thought about calling the crew up to film Amanda reemerging from the woods, but decided the scene would read more pathetic than dramatic.

"A crash?" Jeremy asks. "Do you think it was Amanda?"

"No, we only have one car from the fleet up here and it's still in the parking lot," Casey says, biting back the urge to be meaner. The Catch isn't exactly a Rhodes scholar.

"Mike, a word?" Casey says, turning her attention to the only coworker she has left.

Mike looks at her from across the fire a bit like he's been called to the principal's office but also seems to sense the urgency in her voice. He follows her into the fading half-glow away from the fire, where they can be out of earshot if they whisper, and still keep an eye on the contestants.

"What's up?" Mike says, a little too loudly.

She's got maybe thirty seconds to explain the situation before the girls—and Casey lumps Jeremy into that category—get too nosy.

"Mike, I called Dex. I told him. I think he tried to come up."

"Shit."

Casey holds out her phone so they can ring Dex back together, Mike watching her with growing concern in his eyes, but the call goes straight to voice mail: "You've reached Dex," the light gravel of their boss's voice rings out through the tinny speaker. "*Catch* me later."

Even though he may have crashed his car, it's still a terrible pun.

Mike looks unconvinced.

"How do we know for sure it was Dex? Did he say he was coming up?"

She never imagined Dex would try to drive up here himself after she left that voice mail. But he did seem unusually chipper— and a bit more invested in the show than usual—on the drive up the mountain before Date Night. Coming up on a whim, fully loaded, to try to salvage the night seems weirdly like something he would do, shellfish be damned.

"What do you think that was?" one of the girls calls over to them.

"Was it the cops?" another asks.

"We're going to check it out, OK, ladies?" Casey calls over to them. That'll buy her and Mike another thirty seconds, tops, to settle on a plan before the glorified toddlers by the fire cause even more of a ruckus. They can be so needy sometimes. That's what you get, though, when you cast women who look like supermodels but who have the same level of self-esteem they did when they were metal-mouthed middle schoolers.

Mike turns toward Casey, trying again: "What if someone kidnapped Amanda and took her down the mountain in their own car? Maybe that sound was her. Maybe she tried to get away. Stopped the guy's car somehow. Crashed it."

Casey doesn't want to dismiss Mike too brusquely. Not after last night's still-unresolved tension. But she knows he's wrong.

"It's possible," Casey concedes—*it's not*—"but I still think Amanda's fine. And as for the crash . . ."

Mike interrupts her, stretching the definition of *whisper*.

"You saw the busted latch on her yurt, Case, which I still think we should show the girls so they take this seriously. And there was that hairy guy I saw on the road."

"I hear you," Casey says, hoping that a sympathetic look can act as the apology she doesn't have time to make. "But I promise, Amanda's not dead; she's just dumb. Dumb enough to not be able to figure out the yurt doors. That sound was Dex."

Mike's face falls.

"I need to drive down the mountain and check it out," Casey tells him, keeping her tone even but urgent. "I have to go right now. The 911 operator said someone was on their way but who knows how long that will take on this bumfuck island. Dex might need me. He isn't exactly the best driver, you know that. He's been chauffeured everywhere for the last decade."

"Because his blood is half Scotch?"

In any other situation, it would be a clever bit of banter—cleverer than Casey usually expects from Mike. But not now.

"Mike, listen to me. You stay here. I'm going to go make sure the guy who signs our checks is still alive."

In the corner of Casey's vision, she notices the contestants trying to follow the rhythms of their hushed conversation. It's only a matter of time before they walk over.

"I'm not letting you go alone," Mike says in as loud and forceful a whisper as he can manage, his expression pleading. "What if someone did take Amanda? What if they get you, too?"

Casey sees Lilah-Mae moving away from the group at the fire, taking a few tentative steps toward her and Mike, obviously preparing to interrupt them. They can't litigate all of this. Casey doesn't have time for Mike's chivalrous bullshit. Right now, they just have to get the situation under control without getting the contestants any more panicked than they already are.

"Let me come with you. Jeremy will still be here," Mike offers with a sincerity that makes Casey want to gag.

"Oh, yeah, *he'll* be useful in a pinch," she hisses back, and then softens. "I'll come back with cops if Amanda hasn't reappeared by then," she whispers. "If Dex dies this season, someone might as well kill me. You, too. Babysit the girls. Keep them calm. Tell them I'm getting the crew or something."

Not waiting for an assent, Casey turns and walks off past an advancing Lilah-Mae toward the parking lot.

"Casey!" Mike calls out after her.

She turns around to see his mop of black hair flopping boyishly around his ears, his mouth curled into a frown. How can someone so sexy also be so cute in a moment this dire?

"What?" she asks.

"Be safe."

She turns back around. And as Casey strides off across the clearing, leaving Mike to deal with the contestants, their panicked chattering growing more distant, starlight replacing firelight, she thinks of all the things she left unsaid.

April 3rd, 1972

Dear Maggie,

I like to picture you reading these letters, but I can't decide which thought I like more: You tearing them open right there outside the Mobil station, too eager to wait until you get home. Or you walking down Dennison with them stashed in your backpack, smiling the entire way, and devouring them alone in your bedroom like candy bars. I wish I could be in your bedroom. I wish I could fit in your backpack so you could hide me places where your parents couldn't find me. Maybe I could live under your porch? Might be dirty under there but it's still probably cleaner than Ma's place. Least my house wouldn't be on wheels.

I get really silly when I write to you. I hope you like me being silly. I think maybe I'm just going crazy not being able to do much more than pass you in the hallway. Ever since Mrs. Rippelmeyer found us doing, you know, what we were doing over by Quigley Field, school has been hell. Used to be I'd all but run up the steps, but these days I'm dragging my feet.

I regret taking for granted all those notes I used to pass you in homeroom. I should have made them prettier. I should have drawn you better. Because now that I can only write you once a day, I think so hard about every sentence. Before I hide each letter under our rock, I want to make sure it's perfect. I want every word of this to be worthy of you.

Beautiful Maggie, in your letter back to me, please tell me which you do: Do you read these the second you snatch them up or do you take them back to your room first? If it's the second one, could I ask you to do something silly for me? Could you hide my next letter under your shirt so that my words can be close to your heart the whole way home?

Love,
Kathy

Amanda

manda pries open her eyes and screams.

Someone screams back at her. Then someone else. *The other girls? They're here, too?*

No, it's her own voice bouncing off the wall of a blurry cave, glistening with faint moisture, lit only by an out-of-focus fire that feels close, its heat urging her awake. The echoes of her cry ring shrilly in her head as she strains to make sense of her surroundings. Prone, and glued to the ground, all Amanda can make out are shadows.

Then she remembers.

That hairy thing. That wet Bergdorf mink come to life.

"DEX!"

He wasn't on the mountain with them when she got taken, but for some reason it feels natural to call out to him first. He wears such nice suits when they shoot. Tom Fords. Sharkskin. Slim-fit. Those are the suits of a man in control. Amanda is vaguely aware that her thoughts aren't quite making sense—that something isn't quite clicking with her cognition—but that's probably normal after getting bludgeoned by a wild orangutan, isn't it? She tries to remember her own last name—*Parker*—yes, that's a good sign.

She feels a silence as certain as the stone below her. Every bump, every imperfection in the rock, presses itself into her aching ribs. The ape must have dragged her here, Amanda concludes. Her body feels like it was run through a washing machine with the spin cycle set to high. Her ankles are bruised and swollen, one of her hips on the verge of coming out of its socket, her head throbbing from the blow she sustained at the tent.

"Vanessa?" she attempts, faintly, but Amanda can see now that she is alone.

The tartan-print pajama romper she picked out in case Jeremy stopped by is now in tatters, judging from the draft that whips across her back and causes the fire to flicker.

Wind.

She must not be too far from the cave entrance. Amanda remembers that much from Girl Scout camp. She had gone for three summers in Oregon before they finally let her quit. She told her moms it was because she wanted to stay home and take flute lessons, when in reality she resented her troop leader, who chastised her for gluing badges onto her own sash that she hadn't earned yet just because they were pretty. Is this the sort of random memory that comes back to you when your life is in danger?

Focus, Amanda.

She might not have long before that creature returns. Her fingers still function, as she confirms with a few exploratory wiggles. Hands, too. That's enough to start. Head still swimming, she flattens her palms against the ground, tries to push herself up, and collapses back down, arms buckling, lungs drained from the effort. Maybe it's just as well. No use getting up if she can't even see clearly enough to run. Let her eyes get accustomed to the half-light first. Regain some strength.

For a moment as she clings to the ground, Amanda imagines how Dex will narrate her off the show if no one finds her.

"Ladies, Jeremy, I have terrible news to share. Amanda . . ."

There would be a pause. There is always a damn pause.

". . . has gone missing. The search parties have found nothing. The police have contacted her family. Unfortunately, we have to move on."

It'd be the most-viewed episode in *Catch* history. Fans would flock to the comments section of her most recent Glamstapix photo, the one she posted before production confiscated her phone. She's wearing a white sundress with the caption "Last one before Labor Day"—and they would race to be first to post their remembrances and their RIPs and their broken-heart emojis. But no. This is not how Amanda is going to go: alone in some damp cave after getting abducted by a sentient fringe coat. That photo isn't cute enough to be on the news.

Yelping from the pain that shoots through her body as she pushes off the ground again, Amanda stands at last. Her legs feel like jelly, her clothes are torn to shreds, and the front of her body—which she surveys briefly in the firelight—is caked in dried blood, but she is upright. She takes two cautious steps forward, and although her ankles hurt, they can support her weight. Sprained, maybe, but not broken.

She limps toward the cold draft, praying that the opening isn't too far away. Adrenaline numbs her to the pain of her bare feet slamming against the cave floor as she picks up speed, first grunting, then laughing crazily as she feels freedom growing closer on her skin.

And then she hears the echoes of a mournful yell behind her. A yell that transmutes into an angry roar.

That *thing* must have been deeper in the cave. Risking a glance over her shoulder as she breaks into a run, Amanda sees a pair of yellow eyes burning like lasers out of the darkness as the she-ape leaps over the fire in one bound and barrels toward her, its arms almost dragging against the ground as it leans into a full run, limbs pinwheeling and muscles billowing with each pounding step.

"FUCK!"

Amanda turns back and sprints, grimacing through the pain and gasping for air. She clutches her cramping side with one hand while trying to maintain her balance with the other. But the awful pounding of the thing's steps only quickens. And then there's another deafening sound behind her, so loud it feels like it's coming from inside her own skull.

Keep running.

The opening of the cave comes into view—a misshapen oval of starry sky. Amanda's heart leaps at the sight. The oval bobs up and down sickeningly in her vision as she runs. It's not far. But neither is the hairy hand closing around her ankle like a vice. Amanda falls face-first to the ground, her head slamming against the rock with a crack.

As that thing drags her back into its den, Amanda watches the patch of night sky get smaller. She remembers the summers she spent with her moms out at Joshua Tree: How clear the stars were when you got away from the city lights. How much of the Milky Way you could see at once, an entire galaxy twinkling in your pupils.

At that moment, a shooting star plummets straight across the cave opening, an orange ball that flares up and fades, leaving a lustrous yellow tail in its wake as it disintegrates in the atmosphere. Amanda has taken thousands of photos these last few years, but this may be the most beautiful thing she has ever seen.

She hopes that it isn't the last.

May 4th, 1972

Dear Maggie,

Do you remember that night last August when we drove out to Pinnacle Mountain in my dad's Jeep after he passed out? The night we climbed to the summit and nearly killed ourselves because it was so dark on the way back down? I can't stop thinking about it. Not because we almost broke our necks, or because of the hell I caught when I snuck back home, but because of that hour we spent together looking at the stars.

I had seen the Big Dipper before. But you showed me all the little ones, too: Cassiopeia, Phoenix, Andromeda. My favorite, though, was when you pointed out the one that looks like a big dog—Canis, I think—and you said, "That's Oakley, still begging for your table scraps even though he's in the sky." Maybe you couldn't see because of the darkness, but I cried at that.

"Isn't he getting enough food to eat in dog heaven?" I asked you.

"Still tastes better when it comes from a human's plate," you said, and then you brushed back my ratty hair and you held me and we laughed.

To me, your face that night was as beautiful as the sky. You were gazing straight up and I was gazing at you, at the starlight in your hair *and the sparkles in your eyes. Can I say something silly again? I know you told me to stop asking for permission. I think you will still be this pretty when you're old, Maggie. Maybe even prettier. I'd like to be with you when you are.*

Love,
Kathy

Casey

If Dex isn't dead by the time she gets to him, Casey will kill him.

He knows he shouldn't drink and drive, which in Dex's case means he shouldn't drive, period. It's only gotten worse since the divorce. Sharon being around was the only thing that tempered him, and that happened less and less until finally she had his house and their snotty kid every day except for alternating weekends. The only people Dex still has to be semicoherent around are the flight attendants he sometimes fucks during filming—and that doesn't require very much brainpower.

Casey steers the SUV into its first turn and finds the switchbacks are almost more bracing to take in this direction than they were on the way up to Date Night. The winding road declines at a harrowingly steep grade and Casey doesn't have the patience to shift into a lower gear, especially in an automatic. She rides the brake to keep from flying over the guardrail as she comes out of the turn and speeds down the straightaway. Trees fly past the driver's side window, the black night yawning at Casey from her right.

When she left Dex that voice mail, she thought he'd wake up some crew guy who's too stupid to ask questions—Steve, maybe, or Evan—and get driven up the mountain. He could drink a big bottle of his precious Voss water on the way, sober up, and arrive just in time for Amanda to stumble out of the trees with a sprained ankle and piss all over her pajamas.

Forget Mike's nudist and Lilah-Mae's animal noise. Occam's razor would suggest a simple explanation: the girl did something stupid.

Does no one else remember back in Newport when Casey had to pull Amanda off the prow of the boat while she was trying to take an "I'm the king of the world!" picture? She probably got lost in the woods doing a "Midnight Selfie Challenge" or some other inane social media trend. They really should stop serving alcohol before Date Nights, but damn if it doesn't make for good TV.

The second turn feels smoother—maybe because she's banking into the mountain instead of threatening to careen off the edge of it. On the passenger's seat, her clipboard slides across the slippery leather. A lighter touch on the brake at just the right moment proves to be enough to clear the angle without losing too much speed.

She hammers down the accelerator again. With any luck, the police will already be on their way up the mountain, so, if Dex did crash, they'll spot him first. God, Casey hopes he's still alive. If he only knew what they had put in the can tonight—an F-bomb, explosive taboo secrets, the franchise's first same-sex kiss.

C'mon Dex. Hang in there.

There has been too much work put into this to lose it all now. The fireside moment was literally months in the making. Casey had messaged Vanessa's secret to Lilah-Mae's friend from a burner account a week before filming began—one of many seeds she had planted, and this one is certainly sprouting. Letting Vanessa hear the strategy session on the intercom? That was an inspired touch. The season villain came into Date Night feeling especially feisty. And now the line "you had an abortion *six months ago!*" is going to be in every trailer all season long, teased endlessly but only revealed in the penultimate episode. *If* there is a season.

"Dex, you fucking idiot," she mutters to herself, decelerating to hit the third switchback, but not enough. Casey feels the SUV leaning as she pilots it, hand over hand, through the near 180-degree turn. She's going fast. Too fast. The vehicle groans. The weight of the car starts to lift off the wheel she's sitting over.

Shit, shit, shit.

Casey panics, hits the brake, tries to straighten out the wheel. Her heart slams in her chest. And then gravity reclaims the car again as the tires grip the ground.

"FUCK!" Casey exhales, and then continues zipping down Mount Resilience with a purpose, tires roaring against the asphalt. If she's not careful, she'll be the one who ends up dead. And they can't really do the show without her—at least not very well.

The only actual work Dex has done in the last five years was suggesting the switch from diamond to moissanite engagement rings for the finale episodes, and he only did it so that there'd be more room in the budget for his midtier luxury hotel rooms and his floppy room-service bacon. Other than that, the guy has been on autopilot for the eight years she's known him, pivoting on his mark like an automaton, reciting the same lines he has said ad nauseam for a decade: "Ladies, this is the last corsage."

The fir trees seem to close in around Casey as she drives farther down the mountain, lining the road more tightly, their knotted bark coming alive—almost rippling—under the car's headlights. The only interruptions to this wooden gauntlet are the overlook turnoffs that Casey whips past, focused on her goal.

What if something *did* happen to Amanda? They could write around it, right? They'd have to be careful about how they handled it. Maybe they could do a tribute episode with her family, after they get a payout from the show's insurance, of course. Parents everywhere whose children had died in late-night selfie accidents could tune in on a random Tuesday night in January for A Very Special Episode. But they could still shoot the finale after a production delay, right?

No, Amanda's alive. And Dex is going to be alive, too.

He has to be.

But even as she tries to reassure herself, Casey spots a wreck partway down the next straightaway, illuminated by the twin halogen beams of her SUV.

Shit.

It's from the *Catch* fleet. One of the black sedans they rented is folded like an omelet around a concrete divider on the far side of the opposite lane.

Casey drives as fast as she dares toward it, the SUV's digital speedometer ticking higher: 55, 60, 65. As she gets closer, she sees white smoke leaking from the hood in thin wisps that evaporate as they climb into the moonless sky. The sedan's windshield is shattered, a spray of crushed glass glinting on the asphalt in front of it. Improbably, the totaled car's headlights still seem to be working, although the one Casey can actually see to the right of the divider is stuttering on and off, pointing forward at a crazy angle.

And as she brings the SUV screeching to a halt, her own headlights further illuminating the scene in front of the totaled sedan, Casey sees a motionless body in a blue pullover amid the glass, facedown.

"Fuck."

She throws the driver's side door open, but can't quite bring herself to step out of the car, still frozen in shock. The car beeps to remind her the door is open. That she should go check. But she doesn't want to know what she'll find.

Dex can't be dead. No, no, no. They can patch him up. It might take $20,000 of facial reconstructive surgery before Network ever lets him go on camera again. Sure, his jaw looks loose, hanging open onto the road. Yes, there's still blood trickling from his temples through little grooves in the asphalt, collecting in a shallow crimson pool. But they can patch him up, right? Repair his snapped ribs.

Casey doesn't care if they have to put him in a wheelchair and spin his eventual return to *The Catch* as some kind of inspiration porn. The show can't be over. Not now. Not like this. For a moment, Casey pictures producing Dex as he does the late-night talk show circuit with the story of his car crash—accidental, of course, and not alcohol-related, although the assholes on Catch-Chat will read between the lines.

The studio audience will "ooh" and "aah" with every twist and turn of the story. They can even show a picture of Dex's body covered in casts. In just a second, when she gets out of the car, she's going to take him to a hospital herself and they'll wrap him up like a goddamn Looney Toon.

"Dex?" she calls out, weakly.

There'll have to be a funny ending to the story. Dex's late-night story. Casey can have a writer—a better writer than they have on *The Catch*, for sure—punch it up before Dex does Fallon. Maybe the EMT who comes—who surely must be on his way already—can ask him who's going to win this season and Casey can have Dex claim that, even stretcher-bound, he said, "Find out Tuesdays at eight, seven central."

That'd get a big laugh. Maybe even a ratings spike.

Casey feels detached, almost weightless, as she puts the car into park. It's time. Time to face what can't be true.

"Casey," a man's voice booms behind her.

May 5th, 1972

Maggie,

I know I wrote you only yesterday but I needed to write you again.

I've wanted to say this so many times, but I didn't want to tack it onto the end of another letter. Putting it in a PS would do it a disservice. So while I'm sorry this letter is short, I thought this single sentence deserved its own piece of paper.

I love you, Maggie.

I know I sign my letters "Love, Kathy," but I've never just plain said, "I love you," and I do. I really do. I'm dreading leaving this letter under the rock behind the Mobil because I can't bear the thought of waiting a whole day to hear whether you love me back.

I'm just going to stop writing this now and hide it for you. If you pass me in the hall tomorrow, maybe you can just blink twice. I'll know what that means.

Love,
Kathy

Lilah-Mae

"**S**o we're on top of a mountain," Lilah-Mae sums up, mostly because she finds it hard to believe so much can be going wrong in one cursed night, like the book of Job on fast-forward, "and Amanda is missing. Casey is gone. Mike went to the bathroom and never came back. And we have no phone."

"You solved it, Sherlock!" Vanessa says, clapping sarcastically while glowering at her from across the fire. "Now didn't you say your last prayer twenty minutes ago? I'm still waiting for all your guardian angels to come rescue us."

"Girls, please," Jeremy intervenes. "Let's stay calm."

But of the four of them abandoned on this forsaken peak, Renee is the only one who looks like she's willing to heed that advice. She is sitting on a stump by the fire, staring deep into the coals. Does she not care about any of this? That wouldn't be much of a change, but you'd think multiple disappearances would be enough to get a reaction out of her.

Earth to Renee: everything is falling apart.

"Jeremy's right," Lilah-Mae says. "There are bigger things happening right now than you and me, Vanessa."

In a way, Lilah-Mae is actually glad Vanessa revealed her secret on camera. Her employment history has haunted her for three years now. She erased all of her old social media profiles after Baylor—the ones where she'd covertly post pictures of herself in her uniform. And now, on Glamstapix she always spoke in generalities about being converted after leaving a "period of darkness" behind. She was worried that her followers wouldn't take her seriously as a devout Christian if they imagined her in that form-fitting cotton tank top—that it would make her sins too concrete for them.

Better to let them picture her going a little too far with a high school boyfriend than putting her butt in some businessman's face for a bigger tip.

But she can use this revelation once it airs on TV. Lately, everyone on Glamstapix seems to want authenticity, honesty, and transparency. They want access to the "real" you: raw, unvarnished, unfiltered. Lilah-Mae can probably get credit for being forthcoming. And what better way for her to prove how cleansing the blood of Christ can be than to share how far she fell before He raised her back up, before He swept away her sins like the morning mist washes away the night.

She can have what so many other Christians with large Glamstapix platforms lack: A narrative. A story. The most powerful one of all: *I once was lost, but now I'm found.*

But she won't get to tell that story if there isn't a show to tell it on.

"Bigger things?" Vanessa balks. "Bigger things?! You're not going to get death threats for working at fucking Hooters, L.M.

What do you think all those Waco whack jobs in your home state are going to do to me when I become the *Catch* contestant who had an abortion?"

Vanessa turns to Jeremy, who is looking down at his feet, hands shoved in his jean pockets, clearly uncomfortable with the girl's outburst. She hooks her arm through his.

"Don't you think she went too far, babe?"

Jeremy grimaces and pulls away.

"I think Lilah-Mae's right. Now's not the time."

"GAH!" Vanessa lashes out at him. "What is wrong with you tonight?"

The firelight flickers across the lines forming on Vanessa's forehead, her whole face twisted into an angry knot. Lilah-Mae never noticed it before, but Vanessa is ugly. Like, really ugly. That's what spite and anger can do to a person. And that's why the light of Christ makes everyone beautiful, even the women with big noses or the women who have a little something extra. In the Bible, they call it a person's "countenance," which doesn't refer to whether or not you're hot—although that certainly helps on Glamstapix—it means how you *wear* your spirit, whether you're visibly burdened by sin or buoyed up by the grace of God's glory.

But instead of hating Vanessa for her ugliness, L.M. just feels sorry for her. Here is a girl who has no other meaning in life besides this man. Lilah-Mae wanted Jeremy *for* something. Vanessa just wants him, period, trying to fill a void inside her that only faith should fill.

"So, what do we do?" Lilah-Mae says, deciding to ignore Vanessa's anger for now.

It's a question none of them has had to ask before. Casey is the closest thing *The Catch* has to an omniscient being and she's not here right now.

All this time, they thought that the producer had everything figured out. That there was some inherent ability she had to keep the show going smoothly. But now Lilah-Mae can see that Casey is just a girl, just like them. She didn't know how to handle Amanda being gone any more than they do. There are no safety rails on *The Catch* anymore. They're just people. Just people, but with cameras—and now even the cameras are off.

"I can't believe this," Vanessa fumes, starting to pace anxiously now that Jeremy has shaken off her arm. "I thought this was a major network production, not fucking PBS. And where the fuck are the cops? When are they going to get here?"

Lilah-Mae looks at Vanessa, who briefly glances back at her. The loathing painted across the shorter woman's face is strong as ever but in her pained expression, Lilah-Mae senses a subtle and unexpectedly conciliatory note.

If Jesus was able to forgive the Roman soldiers who crucified him, maybe she can forgive Vanessa. Honestly, it's hard to be mad at her when she's like this. She acts tough, like so many short girls do, but the second Jeremy distances himself from her, she becomes almost pitiable—a slashing jaguar one moment, a mewling kitten the next, her aggression so easily giving way to desperation.

"I'm sick of standing around this stupid fire," Vanessa says, turning toward Jeremy and gesturing over her shoulder at the observatory. "I'm going to that tower. Maybe I can see the cops coming from up there. Or headlights or sirens—*anything*." She reaches a hand over to paw pathetically at Jeremy's jacket. "You'll come with me, right, babe?"

"Uh . . ." he starts to say as Vanessa eyes him expectantly.

But then Renee stands up from the fire almost at random, oblivious to the group's rhythms and governed instead by some unseen internal mechanism, like a kitchen timer going off. Maybe she's finally ready to rejoin the land of the living.

"I'm going to go look around Amanda's yurt," she announces, plainly, not waiting for anyone to give her the go-ahead.

"Renee, I don't think you should . . ." Lilah-Mae warns.

"Oh, let her go, L.M.," Vanessa says. "It's not like she gives a shit about any of this anyway."

"But she really shouldn't be alone," Lilah-Mae insists.

"I'll go with Renee," Jeremy says.

Vanessa's olive skin goes pale. She looks like she's been stabbed. "What?!"

"Well, Renee can't go alone," he offers, taking a step away from Vanessa.

"Fine," Renee huffs, visibly annoyed at his offer of protection. She clenches her hands tight as she starts to walk away. "But we're leaving now," she calls back over her shoulder, then adds, almost sarcastically, "Bye!"

A stunned Jeremy starts scuffling after her, not bothering to look at Vanessa for permission she would never give him anyway.

"Jeremy!" she calls out, but to no avail.

And then Vanessa is left standing across the fire from Lilah-Mae, betrayal competing with rage for real estate on her face. Is that the sheen of a tear in the corner of her eye? Could it be? No.

"God, he makes me so mad," Vanessa says, looking off in the direction of Jeremy's increasingly quiet footfalls. "Gah!"

Lilah-Mae knows she's going to regret proposing what she's about to say next, but as much as she would like to be free of Vanessa's whining, she doesn't relish the thought of running after Renee the zombie either.

"Vanessa, I know you told me to never speak to you again, but I'd go with you to the tower. We don't have to talk."

Vanessa appears to take that suggestion a bit too literally, falling silent. Of course she wouldn't want to go look around with her. Lilah-Mae just exposed her immorality and promiscuity in front of the entire country. And her so-called boyfriend just brushed her off for someone who's practically been a mannequin all season.

But then Vanessa smirks.

"Fine," she says curtly. "But no Bible talk."

Lilah-Mae laughs, more from the shock of Vanessa's acceptance than anything else. "I'll try."

There's a Psalm that says wrath "leads only to evil" that Vanessa would do well to bear in mind. It's the first of many verses Lilah-Mae suspects she'll keep to herself as they walk off together toward the tower to look for sirens in the night.

Casey

"Casey, it's me," the deep voice behind her finishes saying, and when she recognizes who it belongs to, she barely manages to stop the scream forming in her throat.

Mike.

She whips around to see his shaggy crop of hair poking up over the far rear row of seats. He must have stowed away in the trunk. It would be a pretty bumpy ride back there, but Mike is strong enough to brace himself against the twists and turns.

"Shit, Mike," she hisses. "I told you to stay with the contestants. How did you . . . ?"

The car continues beeping to let her know the door is still open. That Dex is out there, probably dead.

"It's fine," he says, clambering over the back row, pushing his hair out of his face as he plops onto a seat. "Jeremy's with them. I couldn't let you go alone. I told them I was going to the outhouse. Had to run, but I beat you to the car while you tied your shoes. Snuck in the trunk with my key."

Casey stares at him, unable to form words, gesturing dumbly over her left shoulder at the windshield.

Mike follows the gesture and his eyes go wide. "Shit, is he . . . ?"

"I don't know, I just got here," Casey says, her heart pumping. "I mean, *we* just got here."

In truth, Casey doesn't know how long she sat frozen, staring vacantly at Dex's body, before Mike startled her. But she can't look. Not yet. She's found the one production task that she can't handle herself.

"Goddamnit," Mike says, pushing his hair back, the exhaustion washing over his face. This show is Casey's baby, but she knows that to him, it's just a job. A lot of the other camera guys are pretentious nerds who think they're going to be David Fincher's DP one day, but Mike has always been just barely smart enough to realize that reality TV is the bottom of a very tall ladder.

"I'll go check," Mike says.

And before she can say anything, he's scooting between the captain's seats in the middle row and out the side door, shutting it behind him. She fishes the cell phone out of her windbreaker pocket. No service.

Great.

So much for getting an EMT up here if Dex by some miracle turns out to be alive. But he's not, is he? Casey takes the keys out of the ignition, then pulls the driver's side door back shut, as though closing it can shield herself from the awful knowledge that's about to come. The bent headlight sends Mike's shadow slanting in improbable directions across the road as he walks toward the wreck. Then he is over Dex, staring straight down at his body.

Casey tries to read the emotion on Mike's face from ten yards away: is that grief, she sees, or just stress? Exasperation, maybe, over the fact that his boss's bad habit has exploded all over this winding mountain road in a spray of blood, glass, and viscera.

Mike crouches down, gingerly puts two fingers on the side of Dex's neck, looks up—right at Casey—and shakes his head.

And finally, Casey cries, a single gasping sob escaping from her mouth, followed by gasping jags. Just hours ago, when they talked strategy in the car, it was almost like she was talking to the old Dex. The Dex she heard stories about from the people who trained her in 2011.

And now Dex Derickson is dead. Worse than dead, he's road-kill. Of course he didn't survive. How could he have?

Judging from how far he flew, headfirst, through a windshield, he must have hit the divider between the road and the overlook turnoff going well north of seventy miles per hour uphill, which means he was drunk, not that it was ever in doubt. Casey looks up through the moonroof at the swath of night sky above her, hemmed in by treetops on either side, her tears blurring the stars into a thousand streaks of light. She can almost see it happening: the car getting cleaved in two by the concrete divider, the windshield shattering around Dex's skull, then him flying through the air like a rag doll before landing facedown with an ugly, fleshy thwack. Such a perfunctory end for a man millions knew and who, despite all his imperfections, gave Casey a life.

Now that man is gone.

Wiping her tears, she looks back down at the scene to find Mike still crouched over the body, staring intently at the shallow crimson pool of blood collecting near Dex's head.

What is he still looking at?

That's when Casey spots it, too. She has to slide forward and crane her neck over the dashboard to get a better angle on the scene. Mere feet from where Mike is crouching, there's what looks like a bloody footprint. And to the left of it, another. And another. Casey follows Mike's gaze to the still-wet tracks that lead from the body toward the concrete barrier that crumpled Dex's car like a soda can.

No, no, no.

Casey has a feeling of premonitory dread. Like she should burst out of the car and say something. She opens the door again, but finds herself frozen in place. Mike is already following the footprints, taking care not to step on any of them as he treads toward the concrete divider. He's walking slowly, his boots scraping against the street. And then the quiet becomes a noise in itself: a pregnant silence that rises to a static roar in Casey's ears. She opens her mouth to shout but chokes instead, her mouth gone dry from the anxiety of watching him move toward whoever—or whatever—left those footprints behind.

"Mike," she manages, but in a throaty whisper, audible only to herself.

The cameraman leans over the wall.

"What the fu—?" Mike starts to yell, but he can't finish the question because he doesn't have a mouth by the end of it.

The unmistakable flash of a muzzle and in a split second, Mike's jaw is gone. His face almost ripples from the force, a little geyser of blood spurting out the wound at the top of his skull. He stays standing for a moment, but only a moment, held up by mere inertia, and then Mike—or what used to be Mike—falls backward onto the road, his body reduced to a pile of dense flesh.

A woman, middle-aged, her hair pulled back into a baseball cap, emerges over the wall, a thin wisp of smoke still emanating from the steel barrel of her hunting pistol.

Casey claps her hand over her mouth and tries to muffle her own screaming before ducking down behind the dashboard.

She trembles in place, keenly aware now of each breath.

Quiet. Have to stay quiet.

"Great!" a woman's voice, faint but amused, projects into the night.

Shit. Did she see?

"Just great!" the voice continues.

If not Casey, then who the fuck is she talking to? Casey contemplates her options as the bile rises in her throat. She needs to get out of here—*fast*—but shock has turned her muscles into motionless mass. This is the second dead body Casey has seen in as many minutes—and she could become the third if she doesn't leave. She slumps out of her seat, down to the floor of the SUV—slowly to soften the sound.

"You just *had* to step in the guy's blood, didn't you, Maggie?"

Maggie? Like from the B&B?

It has to be. But why the hell would that old lady want to help kill a *Catch* cameraman? Casey's head is swimming. Her boss is dead. Mike is dead. Did they do something to Amanda, too?

"I said I was sorry, Abigail," another woman's voice calls back.

Abigail.

Casey feels like she's heard that name before, but right now, it hardly matters. She needs to move. They'll find her. If they haven't already, they'll hear her if she starts running. Out here, in the unearthly quiet, any sound would carry in an instant, like a basketball in an empty arena. Should she drive back up the mountain? Risk getting shot as soon as she puts her foot on the gas?

No, she can't K-turn on this narrow mountain road without giving the shooter a full minute to fire into the car and she can't drive past them either. She'll have to escape on foot. It's the safest way.

Casey rises to a kneeling position between the front seats of the car and, peeking over the dash, sees two women—one silver-haired, the other younger with pinstripe-straight black hair—standing over what's left of Mike, dispassionately examining his corpse.

Who the fuck are these people?

She has just finished ducking back down to the floor when she hears a third voice join the others. "We'll just get Mitch up here to power wash Maggie's footprints and then we can move this guy, OK?"

"It's going to rain in the morning," another voice—a fourth?—joins in.

Fuck. How many of them are there?

"That'll take care of Maggie's footprints for us. By the way, Maggie, quick news flash from the future: we don't wear socks with Birkenstocks anymore."

"It's fall, OK?! How else am I supposed to keep my feet warm?"

These women are fucking insane. But if they keep chattering away like this, she can escape. If she slips out of the car quietly now, she can take off into the forest. They might hear her once she breaks out into a run, but with a head start, she could lose them in the night and get back down to the town by morning. The driver's side door is gaping open, tempting her to escape.

"You're never going to let me hear the end of this, are you?" the woman who must be Maggie whines.

Casey slides toward the door, bending her body so that her torso is hunched over the front seat, ducking down to keep her head out of view. Inch by inch, she scoots toward the opening, the vinyl of her windbreaker scritching against the front seat. If she doesn't exert herself, she won't breathe too loudly. Why aren't they talking anymore? Why aren't they saying anything? Casey freezes, drawing in one last breath through her nose and holding it.

Silence.

"Um, nope, no chance!" someone finally responds to Maggie's rhetorical question, and then they all break out into laughter.

Now.

Now while the laughter can still cover over the sound of her exit. Casey brings her right leg from out below her so she can place it on the ground, but as she does, her left foot slips on something on the vehicle mat. Her face plants against the seat cushion and she struggles desperately to find her footing, looking down between her legs to see what she stepped on. Her clipboard? It must have fallen from the front seat during the hairpin turns.

Even amid Casey's panic, she hears the women's laughter suddenly cease, her heart stopping along with it.

Shit, shit, shit.

"Someone's with him!"

Footsteps race toward her, not just from the direction of Mike's body, but from all around the car.

"Get her!"

No point taking the stealthy route now. Casey launches her body sideways and rolls out of the open SUV door, but she knows that even the old bitch from the B&B will be able to close the gap between Mike's body and the car by the time she hits the ground. Casey lands on the unforgiving asphalt elbows first, footsteps coming in close from every side. She sticks her palms to the ground and starts to push herself up when a foot pressing hard on her back sends her slamming back down. The sudden weight on her spine, like an elephant sitting on a balloon, drains her lungs in an instant.

Casey looks up to see if she's got any runway ahead of her—as if she even has the breath to try to run—and sees the gun barrel pointing down at her face. Behind it are not just two women, but five, six, maybe more, standing over her. Beyond them, the darkened trees stand resilient, almost as if they are allied with this deranged posse.

"Please stop moving, Casey," Margaret Davies instructs her.

Casey isn't sure she could move if she tried.

Renee

enee can feel her heart beating steadily and unhurriedly in her chest. The piney mountain air soothes her lungs, penetrating deep inside her body with each breath, filling her with an invigorating sense of lightness. Under different circumstances, this would be a lovely late-night walk under a star-filled sky. Actually, under these circumstances, it still is. Even the stone tower in the distance emits a certain kind of calm, as though it's a talisman watching over her, protecting her.

If only Jeremy weren't here.

She is following close behind the Catch as he walks away from the fire, away from the stone tower, toward Amanda's yurt at the far west edge of the clearing.

Renee wasn't all that surprised when he jumped on the chance to come with her after she announced that she wanted to poke around for some answers. After all, Lilah-Mae was being a bit much with all her thoughts and prayers—even for her—and Vanessa, as hot as she was, was "as clingy as a pit bull"—Jeremy's words, not hers.

But Renee can barely stomach being alone with the guy and his dumb pomaded hair. The synthetic rustling of his puffy vest cuts through the silence of the otherwise still fall night. This season of *The Catch* is over. That much is clear. A missing contestant and what sounded like a car crash are far from minor hiccups. But Renee seems to be the only one capable of acknowledging that. Vanessa is still hung up on Jeremy, who is actively trying to get away from her. Lilah-Mae wants things to go back to normal so she can get more screen time, probably. And Casey—Casey just wants to keep her job so badly she was willing to go off searching by herself. Renee doesn't know how much the producer gets paid to emotionally terrorize influencers and scout bottom-of-the-barrel bachelors, but it can't be worth this, can it?

Jeremy's boots thump against the rock, echoing across the clearing.

"We're getting close!" he calls back to her, turning around expecting to find . . . what?

Renee full of adrenaline? Ready to play action hero like he has apparently decided to do after acting like a little chickenshit during every physical activity—mountain biking, basketball, bungee jumping—all season long? No, Renee knows that whatever has happened is fait accompli at this point. She can feel it.

"How are you so calm about all this, Ren?" Jeremy asks, walking backward for a moment before coming to a halt, forcing them to talk face-to-face.

Ugh.

He wants to have a conversation. Now of all times.

"I'm calm, *Jer*," Renee says, "because this show is finally over."

Renee can barely stand to look at this man. The way he makes his greasy widow's peak stick straight up, the idiotic expression on his face like he's trying to read a book in a language he doesn't speak, the pride with which he carries himself, as though he weren't a patently ridiculous human being—everything about him is so very tedious. Did he want to come look for clues about Amanda or did he want to waste her time gabbing about reality TV?

"What, because Amanda got lost in the woods and somebody *maybe* had a fender bender? Nah, this thing isn't over yet. I'm not sure why you'd even want it to be. You'll get to stay at the best hotel all season, plus you'll get that Glamstapix boost for being runner-up. I could maybe talk to my co-founder about upping your follower count even more, too."

Renee laughs almost as if for an audience—an audience of the towering trees that encircle the clearing. How refreshing it is to be performing only for a forest, only for the sky. If Amanda is out there somewhere, waiting to be found, Jeremy apparently thinks *this* is more important than she is. Renee has finally had enough of this man's bullshit and, at long last, there are no cameras around to stop her from telling him exactly how she feels.

"*Glamstapix?* You think I give a shit about your stupid app? You give me corsage after corsage this whole season, knowing the entire time you don't really want me to be here, just to get your gold star for keeping the Black girl for so long. And you expect me to just go along with it?"

Jeremy looks bewildered. And yet a smirk forming at the corner of her mouth tells her he knows that she's right.

"Look, Ren, if I had my way, I would have sent you home during week four. I'm only taking you to the finale because Casey told me I had to."

"Fuck you, *Jer*," Renee says, almost throwing the words away because at this point he's not even worthy of her invective. "As if I'd want you to pick me anyway."

She walks past the moron in front of her and takes off toward Amanda's yurt—a dome in the middle distance, just barely visible in the starlight. She has things to do. She can't be bothered with the Catch anymore. If she's being honest with herself, some part of her—a twisted part, maybe, but an honest one, is hoping to find out that something terrible happened to Amanda after the Truth or Dare game. After she humiliated her in front of everyone. After she stomped on her heart and laughed about it and high-fived her friend to celebrate. It's a thought that feels delicious to embrace, like finishing off a pint of ice cream instead of returning it to the freezer.

Behind her, she hears no movement. Jeremy is still rooted in place.

"Maybe you would have rather gone home with Amanda?!" Jeremy bellows after her. "You kissed her *way* better than you ever kissed me!"

"That's because you taste like unwashed asshole, Jeremy," Renee calls back over her shoulder, still plowing ahead, not wasting any time.

She's getting close now. Close enough to barely make out the canvas flap of Amanda's yurt yawning open, flitting slightly in the breeze.

Behind her, she hears the thudding of Jeremy's boots. His pace quickens as he tries to catch up with her.

"I don't know a lot about reality TV," he calls after her, "but I don't think dykes are supposed to go on *The Catch*!"

It really is always the most insecure men who snap like this, who can't bear the thought of even one woman not wanting them. The yurt is close now, twenty yards away.

"Maybe after I pick Amanda in the finale," Jeremy shouts, his voice growing closer, "we'll let you be our third!"

Renee reaches the yurt and spots something almost instantly in the faded glow of the yurt's hanging entrance lamp: a shred of tartan-print cloth stuck to a shrub between two boulders. She recognizes it immediately because she thought the Christmassy romper looked cute on Amanda when they roomed together in Newport. Back when she cared about Amanda looking cute.

Whipping around, she finds Jeremy red faced and panting. She knows he wants the satisfaction of a fight, to feast on her wounded feelings, but she is past all that now. The stars are shining over them by the thousands, an otherworldly reminder of the television viewers that all of this was ostensibly for, except unlike Nielsen sets, the lights in the sky are silent and permanent, completely unmoved by the proceedings below. The firmament doesn't care who lives or dies—and Renee suspects there is some wisdom in that stance. If Jeremy wants to insult her, she has one, ultimate edge: she doesn't give a fuck what happens to any of them anymore.

"You might want to make sure your future fiancée is in one piece first," she tells the whining man-child, gesturing over her shoulder in the direction of the torn tartan-print cloth. "That's part of her pajamas on that bush."

And finally, Jeremy, following the direction of her gesture, falls mercifully silent. He pulls out the flashlight that he found in Casey's bag back at the fire and illuminates the red-and-green fabric with its powerful spotlight beam.

He turns to spout out one last bit of venom, "What is wrong with you, you crazy fucking bitch? Something could be seriously wrong with her."

As Jeremy's flashlight beam strays, Renee spots another shred of the telltale fabric behind the yurt on the right side, partway between the tent and the dense greenery lining the edge of the stone clearing.

"There's another piece," she says. "Do you want to look for her or not?"

At last, he relents. The only thing that can distract Jeremy from a wounded ego, apparently, is the fear that he won't be able to fuck Amanda like he wanted to in Palm Springs next week. Their silence as they walk toward the second fabric scrap constitutes a tacit agreement to put Jeremy's insults behind them, all those meaningless words he hurled from his chest with nothing to back them up. Jeremy leans down to pick up the fabric scrap, feeling its texture between his fingers and eyeing it as though he were some kind of animal tracker, not a smooth-handed trust-fund boy who's never had to sweat for his bread.

Jeremy drops the fabric back to the ground.

"AMANDA!" he calls out, but the only answer is his own voice, echoing behind him and muffled by the thick fir trees just ahead of them.

"It looks like they were headed into the trees." Renee states the obvious for him, in case he's too dumb to piece it together. "We should probably look for more signs of her."

As she says it, she can't help but think of Hansel's trail of bread crumbs. At this point in the night, with so many strange things happening, Renee wouldn't be shocked at all to find a gingerbread house in those woods.

They walk wordlessly behind the yurt into the trees, carefully following the beam of Jeremy's flashlight over the broken stones that bleed from the clearing into the understory of the fir forest, giving way to a softer terrain of pine needles and old roots. It smells gorgeous, Renee realizes, all of these trees. These pine needles. This sweet sap.

"Amanda?!" Jeremy tries again. "If you can hear us, say something!"

Some small piece of Renee knows she should feel scared. What if an animal—or worse—took Amanda? Maybe it's the relief of admitting she's done with *The Catch*, or perhaps the residual high of realizing that she can embrace what she truly wants— but Renee feels at ease as she walks through these woods. The crisis has become its own sort of calm. Jeremy, though, looks unsteady, as if the forest is only remaining silent to punish him.

"I don't hear anything," he reports, like it's a helpful observation.

Exactly.

When was the last time she heard nothing? Not the click-clacking of a coworker's keyboard, or the footsteps of her upstairs neighbor, or her phone dinging to let her know there's a two-day flash sale on women's chinos. Just *nothing*. It's the simplest pleasure in the world and yet how far Renee had to travel— on a plane, a car, and one rickety ferry—just to experience it. Otters Island feels like the first place Renee has truly been able to hear herself think. Or maybe the first place she has ever allowed herself to feel comfortable with *what* she thinks. A place where that decaying part of her can be beautiful, like mushrooms growing on a fallen tree.

So much of her has been buried under useless bullshit like onboarding procedures and workplace software shortcuts— ephemera that Renee can't believe formed the foundation of her existence just two short months ago. How can she go back to that world? How do you return to civilization once its artifice has been exposed?

This whole time, Renee thought *The Catch* was fake and the world she left behind was the real one. But they're both a sham, aren't they? *The Catch* is just everything fake about the real world elucidated, exaggerated and laid bare.

At least hell is honest in its falseness.

Jeremy's flashlight swings through the underbrush, passing over a tree root and Renee notices a strange glistening substance, almost like sap, drizzling over and across its gnarled form. In a second, the spot is dark again, Jeremy's beam arcing past it.

"Jeremy," Renee says, pointing at the spot in the dark where she knows the tree root should be. "Look there."

Jeremy shines the beam on the root again, holding the flashlight steady as Renee walks toward it and squats to investigate. She sticks her pinky in the substance, already knowing her fingertip will come back an instantly recognizable shade of crimson. It's blood.

Jeremy's stupid face goes ashen.

"Shit," he says.

Renee stays quiet.

"She could still be alive; maybe she just can't hear us," Jeremy rationalizes, but even as he says it, Renee can tell that he doesn't quite believe it himself, that the obvious is dawning on him at long last: *The Catch* is over. He is irrelevant.

"I'm going to look over there," Renee says, pointing to the west of the blood stain.

"I should come with you," Jeremy offers.

"Please don't," she says, and doesn't wait for a response.

She heads off to the right of the bloody root taking in a deep breath of mountain air as she does. Let Jeremy cling to his flashlight. Renee is happy exploring the forest by feel, navigating through the faint outlines of the trees before her. She walks forward, pressing her hands against the bark of each fir she passes to keep herself from tripping.

"Do you see anything?" Jeremy calls out.

"Nope!" Renee calls back, almost automatically lest he follow her, but while the word is still on her lips, she spies something unusual: a rocky drop-off—though it can't be too high, judging from the height of the trees growing just beyond it—with more blood on top of it, and a soft light, barely perceptible, coming from below. Renee feels drawn to the small ledge, drawn by a need to find out what lies in the most secret of places, to know the unknown instead of running from it.

"Renee!" Jeremy calls again, his voice sounding farther away now. "I think I see something! I'm going to check it out."

Good. Let him go.

The drop-off in front of her is only about ten feet above the ground below it, Renee confirms as she approaches, with sloping paths running down from either side. Carefully keeping one hand on the ground, Renee climbs down the right side of the drop-off, and turns at its base to find the source of the light: a cave opening, with a faint flickering within. It looks almost welcoming.

The interior of the cave is at least ten degrees cooler than an already-cold September night. There's a dank smell in the air, and moisture leaks down one wall of the cave from an unknown source. The cave draws her in deeper. Renee climbs past a knee-high pile of stones to keep going. The light—it must be a fire, judging from the hints of warmth—grows brighter, lighting up the shale ceiling and the cracked stone walls, riddled with crags and furrows. The light brightens as she walks. The temperature rises. The moisture on the wall increases from a drip to a light trickle. Looking over toward the sound of the water,

Renee spots a row of crude clay bowls sitting along the edge of the cave floor, gathering the drizzling droplets.

Someone's living out here?

Renee heads around a bend in the cave and arrives at the fire at last, already imagining some grungy hitchhiker—maybe the one Mike thought he saw in the road—bent over it, roasting Amanda's body on a spit or some other grisly sight. But there's nothing there. Renee walks up close to the fire for warmth. The flame makes the cave feel homey, the moist wall sparkling and iridescent, the shadows like dark curtains embracing the claustral space.

Looking down at her feet in front of the fire, she finds a handful of wildflowers strewn across the cave floor, odd but pretty nonetheless.

After rubbing her arms to steel herself against the cold, Renee keeps walking past the fire, and finds an abrupt dead end.

The firelight is weak here, but it is still enough to illuminate the shapes in front of her. Skulls, tibiae, rib cages. And scattered among them, carabiners, shreds of fabric, and old boots, decades-old—styles Renee has only seen in movies. Renee scans the pile, watching the artifacts get older as they reach the base, but there, at the bottom, so dark with blood that Renee barely notices it at first, is a fresh human head, detached from a body that is nowhere to be found. Her hair is tied in a ponytail, her expression frozen in shock, a layer of blood caking on pale skin.

"Hi, Amanda," Renee says, looking down at the head.

Amanda doesn't speak back, because she's a disembodied head.

Alas, poor Amanda.

Jeremy will want to know that the girl he was planning to propose to no longer has an intact spinal column. Which is exactly why Renee won't tell him. Let these people fumble in the night. Let them feel chaos for once.

A few minutes later, Renee has emerged from the cave, ascended the rocky crag, and walked most of the way back to where she and Jeremy parted ways. She finds the Catch aimlessly shining his flashlight around the roots, looking for more blood or fabric scraps. It's a futile search, although he doesn't know it yet. Renee keeps that knowledge to herself like a treasure.

"Uh, anything over there?" Jeremy asks.

Renee pauses, looks him in the eyes and does what Jeremy has done so readily to her for weeks: she lies.

"Nope. Just more trees."

May 25th, 1972

Dear Maggie,

I read your letter and I'm sorry. I shouldn't keep trying to convince you to leave Little Rock. You're right.

But it was a beautiful summer, wasn't it? It passed soft and sweet and faster than I would have liked. I just thought maybe every day could be like that summer if we went somewhere else. But you're right. I'll figure out how to be with you in Little Rock if I have to. I'll use the little bit of money I saved up and get a place of my own near downtown and you can stop over after work, supposing you don't go to college right away.

The thing is, Maggie, I want more than half of you. And as long as we stay here, that's all I'll get because half of you will still be trying to show your parents and the rest of this town that you're not strange like me. It'd be like getting half a scoop of ice cream or half a slice of pie. You'd still be pretty amazing, of course, the way a half-moon can still light up the whole night sky, but I would always want all of you.

Love,
Kathy

Casey

As Casey marches blindfolded up the mountain road, the business end of a rifle occasionally prodding her in the back, she feels like she's back in AP Calculus. She was the only girl in Math League back at Austin High, a real whiz with sines and cosines, but once integrals entered the equation, she could feel her command over the subject start to falter. Everything else had been so easy up to that point. It was terrifying to feel the numbers slip out of her control, to find herself suddenly in the dark.

It's the same feeling she's having now as she tries to figure out why the fuck an elderly innkeeper and her friends would shoot Mike and take her hostage? Did they kill Dex, too? A few hours ago, everything made total sense. Another *Catch* season was coasting to its conclusion. Now Casey's entire livelihood—her life, too, likely—is at stake. Nothing is clicking. It's like staring at a fucking integral on a chalkboard all over again.

"Keep it moving!" one of the women behind her yells, and she feels the barrel of the gun nudging her in the spine again.

She hadn't noticed herself slowing down.

"If you shout, we shoot," another calls up to her, but Casey has an awful feeling, gnawing away at the pit of her stomach, that despite their motto, they're planning to shoot her anyway.

"If you run, we shoot!" a third woman yells.

She hears their footsteps slapping behind her like some deranged brass band, their awful rhythm sounding against the asphalt as she stumbles forward. Back at the SUV, before they put a burlap sack over her head and zip-tied her hands behind her back, Casey thought they looked like a psychotic book club or something—like women in their forties, fifties, and beyond who maybe got sick of reading about murders and decided to start committing them instead. At this point, that explanation is about as good as any other. Why would this Maggie woman want to kill them when she hasn't even gotten the second half of her fee from Network yet?

If only she could read their faces. Casey's good at that. In her line of work, she has to be. But the sack makes it impossible to gather more information about what they're thinking or why they're doing what they're doing, and not having access to her hands means most of her concentration has to be spent on staying upright anyway.

"What do you want?" Casey asks, keeping her voice down lest they accuse her of violating their primary rule.

The women don't respond. A cold blast of autumn air hits Casey in the chest as a breeze whips down the road, guided by the unseen trees that she can still sense glowering down at her on either side. Her windbreaker isn't living up to its name as the gust sends a chill through her body while her head continues to marinate in her own hot breath beneath the burlap sack.

"Margaret, right? Margaret Davies?" Casey tries again. "Did you want more money? A larger location fee? We can pay you more. I can make some calls . . ."

Casey's offer is interrupted by peals of laughter bouncing off the asphalt behind her, the cacophony of their crowing voices echoing in her ears.

"You think we care about your money?" a woman—not Maggie—asks. Her tone is intense and tremulous, a live-wire edge in her voice.

"Easy, Abby," another woman cautions. "Don't talk to her. You'll only make it worse."

Now that's *Maggie*, Casey realizes.

If it's not money, she has to figure out what else is driving them. The first question she asks every prospective *Catch* contestant during the audition process is the one she needs an answer to now: "What do you care about?" It's a quick way to find out what motivates the girls—even if most of them give stock answers ripped straight out of Hallmark greeting cards: love, family, friends, faith. The kind of words you'd put on canvas blocks in the guest room of a beach house. Of course, if they were actually honest with her, most of them would just say, "Glamstapix." It was always about the followers—fame as fleeting as it was inconsequential.

Casey's footsteps are unbalanced and halting. It's hard to walk in a straight line and ponder the situation at the same time. A strong pair of hands reaches out to correct her direction.

"That way," another voice, deeper, booms behind her.

Casey might have suspected some kind of hit-and-run situation between these women and Dex if they hadn't shot Mike in the fucking head the moment he saw them. Why would they want to add second-degree murder charges to manslaughter?

Plus, the way they said her name when they caught her. That almost makes this all seem preplanned.

"Abby, right?" she croaks, trying to gulp down enough air through the bag to finish her question. "I know you don't want money, but what can I do? Is there anything you want?"

It's the oldest trick in the reality TV trade: get someone talking long enough and they eventually let something slip. Start with whoever talks most. Casey knows she can still get out of this. She just has to do what she does best. She has to produce them.

The grade of the road steepens and Casey tries to adjust to the sustained incline, picking up her feet a few more inches with each step.

"You wouldn't understand," Abigail responds, her voice still full of venom.

Good. She took the bait . . .

"It won't do any good, Abby," Maggie cautions her, the elder stateswoman weighing in once again. "It never does."

This is good. They're fighting.

Divide and conquer can be Casey's new strategy. Abigail will be the wedge. She's pulled this maneuver countless times before. How many times has she had to do something so much harder than this at her job? She's had to chew out a dozen camera guys who try to film *The Catch* like Harmony Korine instead of getting the simple two-shot she asked for. She's sobered Dex up countless times to do one good take before he slinks back to his trailer. She's convinced a hundred hotel clerks in a hundred different cities to disable the Catch's in-room porn channels so that he stays horny for the contestants instead of jacking off to some bukkake bullshit every night with those shitty miniature lotions. She can do this. There's still hope.

"What wouldn't I understand, Abby?"

"Turn here!" the deeper voice interrupts, and then the strong hands grab her shoulders again, pointing her forty-five degrees to the right. Up another switchback? Casey plods forward, dragging her feet, slowing her pace as much as she thinks she can get away with, still waiting for an answer to her question. Her sneakers scrape reluctantly against the asphalt.

"Abby?" she prompts again. The cold barrel of the rifle pushes into the nape of her neck.

Shit, shit, shit.

"Please, please, please," she begs, frantic, her heartbeat pounding in her ears.

The rifle cocks behind her, the click reverberating loud through her skull.

"No, no, no, no, no," Casey mutters. "I'll be quiet."

"It's OK, Mary," Abby's voice says, her tone more even now. "I want to talk to her."

The rifle leaves Casey's neck.

"I wish you wouldn't, Abby," Maggie cautions.

Behind her, Casey hears Abby fall silent for a moment. Then there's a long inhalation. When she speaks, the edge in Abby's tone is gone, and the soothing alto of her voice forms an odd contrast with the sharp staccato of the group's footsteps. She sounds almost like she's uttering a prayer. Like she's given this speech before.

"I saw something here that made me realize that beauty—*true* beauty—exists on a plane apart from life or death or anything else I used to think was so important. That kind of beauty is here. On Otters Island. I wish you could have seen her, too."

The hands grab her again. Point her in a new direction again.

"Who—" Casey starts.

But at that moment, she trips and falls, expecting to hit the asphalt face-first, but instead landing with a soft thud on dirt and pine needles that poke through the burlap sack. Dirt means they're leaving the road. That can't be good.

"Get up," the deep voice demands, and then the hands are pulling her up by her shoulders and shoving her forward, forcing Casey to take a few running steps to keep her balance.

"Where are we going?" she demands, righting herself. "I wouldn't be falling down if you took this bag off my head."

"You're going forward," the deeper voice—Mary, right?—commands.

The strong hands shove her again. She takes more shaky steps forward on the dirt.

"Please don't do this, Mary," Casey begs, out of ideas at last.

Some people can't be produced—and Casey doesn't have the option to send these women home like she would an unmanageable contestant.

"We don't *want* to do this," Maggie chimes in, almost sweet now, grandmotherly, even.

"So why are you?" Casey asks, desperate. Maggie has confirmed it: they're planning to kill her.

"Let's just say you got very unlucky," Maggie says. "If you hadn't come down the mountain when you did, you could have left."

"No, let's not 'just say'!" Casey says, her voice faltering as her frustration crescendos into a full-blown shout. Let them shoot her. They're going to anyway. "If this is about the camera guy you shot, I promise I won't tell anyone! And if you had anything to do with the crash, I won't tell anyone about him, either. I don't give a shit about them. Can't you please just let me leave?"

And then Casey weeps into the stuffy bag tied over her head, taking choking breaths through the burlap. She has gotten dozens—probably hundreds—of contestants to cry over so many little things, like who stole whose Dyson Airwrap from whose hotel room. Now it's her turn. Apparently this is what it takes: seeing Dex and Mike dead and being marched to her death by some lesbian death cult.

She slows her pace after nearly tripping on what feels like a tree root.

"We can't let you leave now, Casey," Maggie says. "We have to protect this place."

"You need to protect this *island*?!" Casey screams. "Your dusty knickknacks and your mildewy hotel rooms and your . . . fried clams?! *That's* what you're trying to protect? We only came here because we're so fucking cheap. We're only here because no one else wants to be!"

But even as she tries to sound defiant, Casey feels something else, quieter, sinking slowly to the bottom of her gut: a panging realization that she will not live long enough to look back on her life's work. If anyone had ever asked Casey the same question she asked every auditioning contestant, her answer would be this show, every time. This dumb but beautiful, mind-numbing but captivating, loathed and loved TV show. *The Catch* is as complex and strange as advanced calculus and goddamn it, Casey loved it, headache though it was. Her anger at the women is already fully tilted toward despair as Abigail's voice sounds close behind her.

"I knew you wouldn't understand," Abigail whispers, close in her left ear, and then a hand, smaller than Mary's, pushes her forward again, weaker but still insistent.

Onto wood? Yes, the texture below the soles of Casey's shoes has changed. Her footsteps are echoing differently now. The space around her sounds more open, like the trees have gone. She hears water nearby, lapping somewhere below her feet. There's a vaguely sour smell in the air.

Oh God. No. No, no.

"Don't do this!" she screams.

But the women don't obey. They don't have to obey. They're not contestants. They don't want anything from her. No one is going to follow her orders anymore.

"I wish you could have seen her," Abigail whispers again.

"PLEA—" Casey starts to scream, but then she is shoved forward again and she's falling, falling into the water she already knew would be below her.

The water is ice-cold, instantly soaking through Casey's windbreaker, shocking her into motion. She thrashes, pumping her feet trying to keep her head above water. Behind her back, she strains against the zip ties, struggling to pull them apart, hoping for superhuman strength but realizing that she is all too human. The only sound she hears is her own futile splashing and churning—the sound of the inevitable being delayed. The women must be watching her in silence.

Still, she fights. With every ounce of energy she has left, she fights to live. And then her strength gives out and Casey is sinking, the weakening thrusts of her feet no longer enough to keep her body afloat. The water comes seeping in through the burlap, gripping her face with a thousand frigid fingers. It pours into her airways as she tries to scream, flooding her lungs.

She has reached her own personal season finale.

Vanessa

"**L**adies first," Vanessa says, gesturing toward the opening at the base of the stone observatory, a gaping rectangle of blackness that neither girl is eager to enter.

"You're a lady, too," Lilah-Mae protests.

The looming tower, intimidatingly tall when viewed from such a low angle, takes no position on their standstill. It simply thrusts into the star-dotted sky, impassive, apathetic to the catastrophe of this night. There's a permanence to the structure, as if the island itself has grown out from underneath it, pushing it upward in the process. The hand-cut stones it was constructed from are well-worn, polished round and smooth by a century's worth of wind and rain.

Back at the campfire, this seemed like a good idea. Now, Vanessa's not so sure. But L.M.'s already seen her sweat enough tonight.

"As you wish," Vanessa says, then tries to hide the trembling in her legs as she takes her first step inside.

The temperature drops from its already nippy autumn low as the interior of the tower wraps around Vanessa, enveloping her in its shadows. The ceiling is a mere six feet or so high, the stairs not even wide enough to walk two abreast. The steps themselves are set at a jarringly high grade. Vanessa nearly trips on the first one.

She almost wishes she and L.M. could have stood outside the tower entryway forever, fighting over who should go in first. Some vigorous bickering with the ex-beauty queen could bring some sense of normalcy to this nightmare. Anything to not be here, wordlessly climbing steps so tall only an NBA player could scale them comfortably.

Their footsteps fall into a steady, almost syncopated rhythm, Vanessa's landing on the half-beat between Lilah-Mae's. Thump, *thump*, thump, *thump*.

Vanessa counts them: every ten steps they reach a landing, and turn ninety degrees to climb ten more. The tower seems almost eager to ferry them to the top. Vanessa had suggested climbing it, mostly to do something—anything—but ultimately she is realizing that what they'll find at the top of the observatory is beyond their control: The cops are either coming or they're not. Amanda is OK or she isn't. And Jeremy? Well, Vanessa thought there was something special between them—hell, an hour ago, she was sure she'd marry the guy—but now he's pulling away every time she tries to get close and he ran off with Renee to boot. And without him, there's just the wilderness and a bunch of girls, one of whom would burn her at the stake if it were still Puritan times.

Why did L.M. have to say that?

In the back of her mind, she always thought the other girl understood the rules of engagement. Their feud was mostly for

show, wasn't it? Sure, they went at each other off camera sometimes, but mostly to keep the tension up. What was the term?
Method acting? Neither of them were supposed to actually ruin
the other's life.

Vanessa rounds the fourth landing, climbs two steps, and realizes she no longer hears the patter of Lilah-Mae behind her.
She turns around to find L.M. two steps down, panting, her face
pale. The pupils of her eyes are dilated, even more than Vanessa
would expect them to be in the darkness. She looks terrible, like
the tower has sapped her soul out of her body.

"L.M.?"

Lilah-Mae says nothing, but then her pupils roll backward,
her knees buckle, and she starts to teeter back into the gaping
inky blackness of the stairwell behind her. Quickly, Vanessa
steps down, hooks her elbows under the other woman's armpits, and pulls her forward, laying her down as softly as she can
manage.

"Lilah-Mae?"

Her eyes are still open, but fluttering, and her skin is clammy.
Vanessa reaches out and taps Lilah-Mae's cheek with her forefin-
gers, then again, harder. She has always wanted to slap Lilah-Mae,
but not to keep her from fainting. "Stay with me, L.M."

The other girl gulps in air, wrenching herself back into con-
sciousness.

"Whoa," she says, sounding hoarse. "Guess I needed to catch
my breath."

Vanessa could use a break herself. They sit together on the
cool stone of the landing, breathing in deep. Vanessa feels her
heart slow in her chest and notices the ache forming in her legs.

"How high up can this thing go?" she asks.

"Seriously," Lilah-Mae says, wiping some sweat off her brow with the back of her hand. "It's like the Tower of Babel. Sorry. I promised no Bible talk."

Vanessa just rolls her eyes.

"Think we'll even be able to see anything from the top?" Vanessa asks.

"Maybe not, but at least it's exercise, right? I guess it's leg day." Vanessa is unimpressed by her attempt at a joke.

"And if someone did take Amanda," Lilah-Mae continues, "this is probably the safest place for us to be right now, not out there in the open or over by her yurt. I don't know what Renee was thinking."

"Same," Vanessa agrees. "I really hope Amanda's OK and all, but I'm not trying to get Ted Bundied out here."

A few minutes later, after assurances that she feels well enough to continue, Lilah-Mae stands and starts treading up the stairs behind Vanessa, this time at a more even pace.

They ascend together in silence and Vanessa resumes her count: landing five, landing seven, landing ten. Around the next bend, she feels a torrent of cold air rushing down the stairwell, washing away the dank, stagnant miasma she has been breathing the entire climb.

"We're almost at the top!" she says.

Vanessa quickens her steps, leaping up the last flight of stairs two at a time, despite their imposing height. At last, she reaches the top: a square patch of the same hewn stone that forms the tower's walls, about twenty feet across, with a railing around each side.

"L.M.?" she calls out, looking back at the stairwell. Maybe Vanessa should have had her walk in front.

But then Lilah-Mae appears, the armpits of her white shirt soaked with sweat, even in the cold. She doubles over, breathing in deep to recover from the climb.

"Do you see anything?" Lilah-Mae asks, panting, then joining Vanessa by the railing.

"Not yet."

The women patrol the perimeter of the square together, scanning the landscape below for any signs of headlights or sirens speeding their way up the mountain. Nothing. Below one side of the tower, Vanessa can see a gnarled, sinewy tree climbing its way up from a crack in the stone clearing below, but it stops short less than halfway up, its limbs reaching for but forever failing to grasp the turret.

"There's nothing there," Vanessa says, turning to face L.M., who meets her eyes with an unusual softness.

"Hey, um, thanks for catching me back there," Lilah-Mae says. "I could have really hurt myself falling down those stairs."

Is she trying to make nice? No, it's not OK what she did. They can't just move on from it. Lilah-Mae revealed her deepest secret in front of a future audience of millions. The stigma of that moment is likely to follow her forever. Lilah-Mae did that. She did it. Sure, Vanessa has been hard on Lilah-Mae all season long, and the Hooters reveal might have been going a bit too far. But Lilah-Mae's not going to get mail bombs for wearing orange polyester shorts the way Vanessa might for having terminated a pregnancy.

"It wasn't OK," Vanessa says at last, too angry and hurt to look Lilah-Mae in the eyes and casting her gaze out into the night instead. "What you said about me."

Far off in the distance, Vanessa can barely make out the lights of the island's small downtown, a faint imitation of the dazzling blanket of stars overhead. A tear drips down her cheek that she discreetly brushes aside with her pinky. She can't believe she's crying—that *L.M.* of all people has made her cry.

"I know," Lilah-Mae says.

Huh?

"My faith is my faith but I know it wasn't OK, Vanessa. I'm still mad at you for bringing up my Hooters thing on camera but biting back at you like that was wrong. I should have 'turned the other cheek,' like you said on the ferry."

Vanessa can't help but laugh at the callback, though it makes the tears come down in earnest now, as if the only thing holding them at bay was her refusal to let any emotion at all rise to the surface.

"I didn't *want* to get an abortion, you know," she says. "I don't regret getting it—I'm glad I did—but it's not like I set out to do it. I don't want it to follow me forever and now it might. Because of you."

She pauses as a wave of self-consciousness washes over her. It's weirdly relieving to open up to someone, but still, this is Lilah-Mae she's talking to—the queen bitch of Christian Glamsta. Vanessa wipes more tears away and collects herself.

"I don't know why I'm telling you this," she says. "But I'm just . . . I don't know, a fucking person, OK?"

Lilah-Mae takes a step beside her, leaning against the waist-high stone railing, and the two women look out over it together. Everything is calm. No headlights are winding up the mountain. There is no chattering over by the campfire. They're alone—truly alone—for the first time in two months.

Lilah-Mae sighs. A chill wind whips across their faces. The gnarled tree below them creaks as the wind catches its bare limbs, pushing them toward the tower, a couple of the longer branches, outstretched like wooden tendrils, managing to scrape its side. The night sky seems to take a breath along with them.

"Do you think everyone's going to turn up OK?" Lilah-Mae finally asks.

Vanessa debates how optimistic she should be, but settles for the truth instead.

"Not really. I thought it was nothing at first—a bid for attention—but now I'm not so sure."

"Do you think there's going to be a show still?"

"I don't know," Vanessa says. "Maybe not."

"I know it's wrong to say, because there are obviously bigger concerns right now, but I really wanted this to go well. I know you make fun of me for doing them, but all those pageants were for my parents. *The Catch* felt like something that was just for me."

For the first time, Vanessa feels like somewhere in there, underneath layers of Bible verses and clichés ripped straight out of a youth pastor's repertoire of sermons, is a human being. Two months of goading didn't bring out anything authentic from Lilah-Mae, but now here she is. They were all trying to get somewhere. They're all heading in the other direction of *something*, aren't they, all of them running? Even a privileged daughter of Dallas like Lilah-Mae. For a moment, Vanessa feels the thrill of a distance suddenly collapsing.

"Maybe we both left behind versions of ourselves we didn't want to be," she offers.

Lilah-Mae turns to face her now, the left corner of her mouth curling up in a half-smile. The wind relents long enough for the quiet atop the tower to become absolute again.

"Maybe," she says. "There's this Bible verse I like that says if you believe in Christ, then the old you passes away and you become a 'new creation.' But I like to think that's not a one-time deal. Like maybe we're always becoming new. It's not a transformation; it's a process."

A number of scathing comebacks pop into Vanessa's mind, some of them heading for her lips automatically, but instead she just says "maybe" one more time, before letting the conversation trail off.

Almost immediately, the silence is interrupted by the sound of scuffling.

"What was that?" Vanessa asks, feeling her skin go prickly.

More scuffling. Closer now. Vanessa turns back toward the railing, tilts her chin down farther, peering along the vertical face of the stone tower. At the sight of the dark shape, every atom in her body tenses up and explodes in unison. There's a shadow scrambling up the side of the observatory, emerging from the cloud of darkness pooling at its base. It's climbing at an alarming rate, a blur of gray limbs hurtling itself upward.

"Look!" Vanessa shouts, but she knows that what she should really do is run. The thing—*it can't be a person, can it?*—could be at the top in mere seconds. It is scrabbling up the tower in a way no human possibly could, probably scaling fifty feet already.

Vanessa notices Lilah-Mae following her gaze and going white at the sight of the thing.

It can't be a person and yet, the closer it gets, the more it looks like a person, albeit an enormous one, jamming its hands and feet into the concave grooves of mortar that run between each row of stone, pulling itself toward the girls with a feverish intensity.

Lilah-Mae lunges for the stairwell, but Vanessa stands dumbly at the railing, transfixed as the thing skyrockets upward, as though it's attached to a fishing wire being reeled toward the top of the tower. It looks . . . *furry?* Like a monkey? Vanessa can just make out its face with beady eyes, receding forehead, and a flowing mane of hair—and then it is mere feet away, deadlocked onto her.

Vanessa tries to will herself to back away. To run. To follow Lilah-Mae down the stairs. But the thing launches itself up the last ten feet of the wall with a final push off of a tiny toehold. And then it is a huge weight on top of her, driving Vanessa backward onto the stone, its strong arms pinning her down with preternatural force.

Hot drool drips from the animal's mouth into Vanessa's as she screams.

"Get off me!"

She tries to push the monster but it has her shoulders all but nailed to the stone and her forearms can only reach so far. Vanessa can barely discern the thing's grotesque form, but in flashes of clarity punctuating her panic, she sees that it's humanlike, but a quarter-turn off—more of a Neanderthal than . . . a woman? Yes, its breasts hang down over Vanessa, heaving as the animal pants, recovering from the dizzying speed of its climb.

In a flash, it all comes screaming to the front of Vanessa's mind: the figure Mike saw on that car ride, the silhouette in the background of the photo Amanda showed her this morning, the sound Lilah-Mae claims she heard by the yurts. It's been following them ever since they arrived on Otters Island.

"Help!" she cries, but she knows Lilah-Mae is halfway down the stairwell by now. Still, the other girl could go get Jeremy and Renee. Maybe a group of them can scare it away.

If it doesn't kill me before they get here.

The thing recoils a bit at the sheer volume of her cry, but remains planted firmly on top of her.

Its leathery palm reaches down toward Vanessa's head—a hand big enough to hook a thumb under her chin while also clutching her crown with its four remaining fingers, almost crushing her skull through the sheer force of its grip. Through the gaps between the thing's thick fingers, Vanessa can see that its face is softening. Almost . . . smiling?

"HELP!" she tries again, with every milliliter of oxygen remaining in her lungs, then thrashes every one of her limbs she can still feel.

At that, the monkey lets out an awful, guttural yell, pulling Vanessa's head upward and then slamming it down onto the stone, hard, with a smack. Vanessa's vision swims. As the thing removes its hand, she gazes up at the night sky, helpless and disoriented. She can't tell which of the stars she's seeing are from the blow and which are real, shining down on her from trillions of miles away as this creature pummels her to death.

She moans, finding she can no longer form words. The ape lifts its head toward the sky and cries again—a terrible image of pain and anger that Vanessa suspects will be one of the last to imprint on her brain. The thing turns down to look at her again with two deadened, flaxen eyes boring deep into her own with a terrifying sentience. A wild animal wouldn't know what it was doing, but this creature . . . it *sees* her.

The wrinkled palm reaches out for her face once again and Vanessa tries to summon the will to do anything—punch, kick, fight, yell—but comes up short on all counts. And then a screaming whoosh of white fabric and extensions comes barreling toward the deranged monkey, somehow managing to knock it back onto the stone floor beside Vanessa before falling to the ground.

Lilah-Mae.

She came back. Why the fuck would she come back?

"Run!" Lilah-Mae screams, her voice tremulous and uncertain, like even she can't believe the stupidity of what she's just done, or that she did it for Vanessa.

Still on her back, Vanessa swivels her aching neck to her right to find Lilah-Mae wedged between her and the animal, groaning from the effort she expended, the disoriented beast thrashing in anger on the other side of her as its feet scramble for purchase on the slick stone.

"Run!" Lilah-Mae calls again, weaker this time.

Vanessa's head is floating and throbbing from the pain, but freed now from the creature's grasp, she manages to stumble to her feet and hobble three steps toward the stairwell. She hears the sounds of struggle behind her and turns to see the terrible thing, standing fully erect now—it must be nine feet tall—holding the other girl by the throat.

"Lilah-Mae!"

The girl's feet are dangling off the ground, a feeble wheezing coming from deep within her esophagus as she struggles to breathe. Her eyes, big with fear, catch Vanessa's for a moment but strangely, despite what must be unimaginable pain, Lilah-Mae softens her expression into something more plaintive and earnest: a plea.

"Run," Lilah-Mae ekes out, forcing the last of the air out of her rattling windpipe.

And then the beast, with barely any effort, lifts Lilah-Mae even higher, the girl's weakened body hanging by her neck now, her feet flailing four feet off the stone. Vanessa stares in disbelief as the hulking thing casually tosses Lilah-Mae from the top of the tower, the girl's limbs rag-dolling as her body flies past the stone railing, out of sight. The creature's roar drowns out Lilah-Mae's fading scream as she falls.

Vanessa turns and for the first time all season, she does what Lilah-Mae tells her to do.

She runs.

June 18th, 1972

Dear Maggie,

Thank you. Thank you, thank you, thank you. I promise I'll spend every day making sure you never regret running off with me. And I'm sorry that I pushed you to leave before graduation. You're right. We'll get a lot further with at least one diploma between the both of us, and I'll get my GED someday once I figure out what a hypotenuse is. Maybe you can teach me and I'll teach you how to write like me. Not that your letters aren't perfect. I cherish each one of them.

But soon we won't have to write any more letters to each other ever again because we'll just be able to say whatever sweet thing we want to say to each other the moment we think of it. My life will just be one long love letter to you, and I'll keep adding new lines until I run out of paper. I hope that won't bug you too much, but I don't think it will. You like when I'm sweet on you, don't you?

I know you're worried about leaving Little Rock without knowing where we'll live. I can't promise you it will be somewhere beautiful like Hawaii, but maybe my dad's Jeep (well, I guess soon it will be our Jeep) could get there if we added some sails to it. I don't know if our home will

be a forest, a desert, or a jungle. But I do know I'll take you somewhere
we can be us. I'd live in a shack in Death Valley if I could hold your
hand there. I'd want to do other things in the shack, too, but I won't
write about them here. Don't want to get too flustered.

I'll see you at midnight at the Mobil on Friday. I'll be parked around
the corner with the headlights off so no one sees. Have your backpack
packed with all your necessities. I won't need a backpack. You're my only
necessity. Then we'll drive to wherever I-40 ends. At least at first. We can
go wherever you want once we get far enough from here. I've never been
out of Pulaski County, have you?

I cherish the thought that everywhere I go for the first time will be by
your side.

Love,
Kathy

Renee

Renee runs toward the clearing, jumping over rocks and roots, heading in the direction of the girls' distant screams. This is her chance to see *whoever* was in that cave, to meet the mystery behind this exhilarating madness.

Jeremy had taken off running as soon as he heard the faraway sounds of distress, but it was easy enough for Renee to overtake him. The man might be muscly, but he's got no endurance. All show, no go. The beam from his flashlight bobs up and down, dissipating mere feet in front of Renee, but it's enough to guide her steps.

"Renee, slow down!" Jeremy calls from somewhere behind her, gasping between syllables. "I. Should. Get there. First."

No chance.

She feels giddy. Electric. Almost every night of her life for eight years, she has known exactly what to expect: takeout and TV, rinse and repeat. But tonight—this beautiful cloudless night—Renee doesn't know what she's going to see except that it's something she has never seen before. Maybe the last thing she ever sees, but at this point, she would welcome an end to all this so long as it was different. New.

She bursts out of the dense trees that surround the clearing. Behind her, she hears Jeremy trip and fall to the ground with an "oof." If he wants to play hero, he's going to have to learn how to balance. The flashlight beam will be gone until Jeremy can get back to his feet, but it's not important. Renee can run by starlight. She starts sprinting across the clearing, her sneakers smacking against the stone.

"Renee! STOP!" Jeremy bellows.

Where was this courage when he wanted to send her home but Casey told him he had to keep her? Where was his chivalry when she was being ridiculed during Truth or Dare?

"HELP!"

The scream is bloodcurdling and sharp, coming distinctly from the direction of the observatory. If she hurries, she can still catch it, whatever it is.

Yes, yes, yes.

Renee begins closing the distance to the tower, charting the most direct course through the sparse scattering of bare trees growing through the boulders below her feet. She listens for Jeremy's footsteps behind her, but doesn't hear any. He probably needed to take a break after skinning his knee, or something.

She runs and runs, panting but persistent. Then she sees it—a sight thirty feet ahead of her so arresting that it stops her in her tracks just as surely as a wall might.

It's almost impossible to process the entire composition at first. A monkey, tall as two saplings stacked on top of each other but with a distinctively feminine figure, is holding a pair of severed legs by the ankles, one in each hand. What's left of a human body is crumpled by its feet. For a second Renee can't help but think of that Goya painting she loved so much before switching her major from art history to English. *Saturn Devouring His Son,* beautiful but bizarre—or was it beautiful because it was bizarre? The thing hasn't noticed her yet, its face still angled off to the side. Renee crouches behind a waist-high boulder to catch her breath and get a closer look.

Behind the beast, Renee confirms, Lilah-Mae is impaled on an upward-curling limb of the bare, weathered pine to the right of the tower, her body gored through the abdomen, slowly spinning like a weather vane on a breezy day. Blood oozes down her body, dripping off her extremities, the little slap-slap of it against the rock below the only sound she's aware of besides the creature's harried breathing.

That must be Vanessa by the creature's feet, Renee realizes. Lilah-Mae still has both her legs.

The magnificent creature starts to swivel her head forward as Renee scoots back behind the boulder.

Did it see me?

A tap on her shoulder. Renee's heart skips and stutters but, of course, it's Jeremy, kneeling down behind her, having taken his sweet time arriving. He must have decided he'd be better off sneaking his way toward the scene than running and giving himself away. His flushed face is full of fright as he wordlessly gestures at the scene in front of them, the switched-off flashlight clutched in a white-knuckled hand.

"What the hell is it?" he whispers.

From the other side of their cover, Renee hears Vanessa's discarded legs landing with a squishy smack against the stone.

"I think it's a she," Renee corrects him.

"Who gives a fuck, Ren, what the fuck *is* it?"

Renee risks another glance around the side of the boulder and spots the ape-woman leaning her long body down, grabbing and lifting Vanessa's torso by the arms. Then, almost absentmindedly, she starts pulling the limbs in opposite directions. The ape's enormous wingspan so vastly outmeasures Vanessa's tiny one, and her strength is so immense, that she can pull the dead girl's limbs out of their sockets simply by stretching her own arms out to their full extension. The sound of muscles ripping and tendons snapping echoes across the clearing. Fluid drips down from the bottom of Vanessa's torso, where her legs were presumably still attached mere moments before they arrived.

Renee turns back to find Jeremy looking queasy, swallowing as if he's trying not to throw up—and he better not, because the splash of his vomit would draw this beast's attention before her work is done.

She peeks back around the boulder's edge.

Vanessa's torso falls to the ground as her arms come clean off in the beast's hands—and then the ape disinterestedly drops the limbs beside her growing pile. A gust of wind whipping across the clearing carries the foul stench of the killing on its back.

Now that she has finished disassembling Vanessa like a Thanksgiving turkey, the beast sniffs at the air and its eyes lock onto the boulder. Renee pulls her head back behind the hiding spot to see Jeremy looking around the other side at the same scene.

This is it. She knows we're here.

A stranger end than Renee imagined for herself but a welcome one. At least she got to see one perfect, incomprehensible thing before she died—something that could raze all her useless memories to the ground.

"It's coming," Jeremy whispers.

"Let her."

Jeremy shoots her a wayward look before rising to his feet. "Hey!" he yells, his upper body plainly visible over the boulder now.

Renee leans again to look. Jeremy produces the small flashlight and shines it right at the lady ape's face.

The first thing she notices under the flashlight's beam is her age. Her body is strong, the muscles beneath her fur bulging out, her frame powerful and lean despite its massive size. She is built with the sort of brute animalistic efficiency that human evolution abandoned millions of years ago—hundreds of times more powerful than any bodybuilder at the prime of life—and yet her stare feels ancient, her forehead wizened and wrinkled, a few gray patches of fur poking up amid the more youthful brown. There is a grace to her, belied by her strength. How long has she been up here? How many decades?

"HEY!" Jeremy roars again, the flashlight quaking in his hand as he does.

The lady ape takes a step back but doesn't retreat altogether, appearing to appraise the Catch with curiosity more than anything else. Jeremy walks out from behind the boulder and steps in front of it, keeping the flashlight beam trained on her face.

"Where's Amanda?!"

The lady ape remains still. Watching. Jeremy scans the ground at his feet, bends over, and pulls a fist-sized jagged stone from one of the cracks between the boulders. The lady ape stays planted in place. On her face is an expression as obvious as it is universal: a smile. She welcomes the challenge. Jeremy grips the rock tightly between his fingers, the skin on his knuckles stretching taut, as he uses his free hand to keep shining his flashlight forward.

Wait.

"Jeremy," she whispers, then louder, "*Don't.*"

But it's too late. Jeremy is rushing at the lady ape with the jagged edge of the rock outstretched in his right hand, ready to attack. He drops the flashlight, its metal casing cracking on stone as it lands.

"Fuck you!" he yells.

Renee knows what to do. She scrambles forward, leaving the cover of the boulder behind, and grabs the cracked flashlight, shining its beam on Jeremy as he runs. Let her see him coming. Let her see the threat clear as day.

"REN?!" Jeremy calls out, but it's too late for him to change course now.

The monkey stands fixed to the spot, Vanessa's blood-soaked body parts at her feet, her muscles tensing as Jeremy finishes his desperate charge. Renee's flashlight remains trained on him close and tight. In a single, hopeless lunge, he hurls himself at the ape, stone outstretched, and the monkey woman turns to shield herself from the attack, catching the sharp point of Jeremy's weapon in its shoulder.

With a yell, Jeremy drags it down her arm before falling to the ground.

Renee watches as blood spurts down from the beast onto Jeremy's glossy pomaded hair. He is lying prostrate, winded from having landed on his chest with his arms outstretched.

She's still standing but the beast cries out—a harrowing, mournful yowl so loud Renee's ears ring.

She's hurt.

"Ren, help me," Jeremy calls over weakly, as he rolls onto his back, wheezing, but Renee doesn't move. She keeps the flashlight steady as the ape woman's thick calves and feet leave the ground, springing upward into a jump.

Renee follows the blur of her motion skyward. At the apex of her leap, she must be nearly five feet in the air. Below her, Jeremy braces for the impact but nothing can prepare him for the crushing weight of the wounded ape as her feet land on his abdomen. Jeremy's ribs crack like twigs, his blood spraying into the night as the beast sinks into him, using his broken body to cushion her landing.

"GAH!" Jeremy cries, a pathetic guttural noise that doesn't belong on the same mountaintop as the beast's beautiful, ancient vocalizations.

Renee watches the hulking mass of brown, mottled fur settle on top of Jeremy, preparing to finish him. He probably can't get up by now. She likely disconnected his spine from his legs with the sheer force of her body weight.

"Renee!" he calls out, desperate, manic. She keeps the flashlight shining on the Catch's broken body as the ape woman lifts her good arm over her head, the other still dripping blood onto Jeremy's shattered frame.

The ape's clenched fist starts to descend.

"Renee, please!" he cries.

He has carried himself this entire season like God's gift to womankind—and now Jeremy is Renee's gift to Her. The ape woman's fist pounds Jeremy's skull over and over, bone crunching under the blows. The man's cries, wet and ragged, grow weaker until they stop.

01/02/18

Dear Katherine,

You always wrote me such beautiful letters when we were young,
so I suppose I should try to write you a good one now that you're gone.
I only wish you were here to read it.

What was so maddening about being with you was that you always
had it much worse than I did, and yet you always loved me better. Even
back in Arkansas, when you were shuttling back and forth between your
dad's house and your mom's trailer, showing up to school with purple
bruises and cigarette burns, you were always more worried about how I
was doing than you were about yourself. You treated me ripping my
favorite pants like a national tragedy; meanwhile, you were dodging
thrown dishes and hurled slurs at home.

You spoiled me, Kathy, is what I'm trying to say. It should have been
me. It's not fair that it was you. It's not fair that even when you were
dying of cancer, you loved me as good as you did.

So let me say again—now that it's too late—that I loved you
ferociously. I loved when you called me "your girl," even after we got old,
and even though I got older quicker than you did. I loved when you

asked me to make you my "special tea." It was just a bit of brown sugar and a kiss of cream, but you pretended like it was a delicacy only I was capable of creating. I loved your rough hands and your smooth body and your innocent face, still babyish and bright even after that godawful chemo. I didn't deserve you, but I loved you and I still do. I'm blinking twice.

Back in Little Rock, you promised to take me somewhere where no one would make us feel the way we did there. And you did. Otters Island has been good to us; and you've been good to it, devoting your life to bringing people here, both for Her and for us. You knew that this place wasn't for everyone, but that it needed to be here for the people who needed to find it. And you understood what She meant to us. People once called us monsters and freaks, too, but I think we were beautiful freaks, weren't we? Just like Her.

Do you remember the letter where you asked me to carry your secret messages home with me under my shirt? You thought it was a silly thing to ask, but I loved it. I'm not sure I ever told you, but I carried every letter you ever wrote me in my shirt after that. The envelopes were sweaty and crinkled when I got to my room, but I did it for you.

Well, I'm going to have Jacky sew this letter—folded up just like I used to fold mine—onto the shirt that we're laying you down in. This time, it's my words that will be by your breast. Carry them home for me.

Love,
Margaret

Renee

She's hurt. The enormous ape is slumped against a boulder, an awful moan escaping her lips and sounding across the clearing. It rends Renee's heart in two to hear it.

The gash Jeremy made in her arm has clearly taken its toll. But she is still alive. Her breasts are heaving up and down slowly, but at a steady rhythm. Meanwhile, Jeremy, or the pulp that's left of him, lies inert on the ground beside the ape, displaced ribs jutting through his abdomen, caved-in head lolled to the side at an obscene angle. The Catch's eyes are still open, staring up into the sky, but seeing nothing.

This is what happens when you try to fight an eight-foot-tall mythical beast. The rock that Jeremy used to slice the lady Sasquatch's arm is still clenched in his lifeless hand, the sharp edge of it coated in fresh blood that catches the light of the flashlight's beam.

There is no sorrow in Jeremy's death, just as there was none in Amanda's, Lilah-Mae's, or Vanessa's. In the grand balance of things, the world can afford to lose them more than it can afford to lose this rare and wondrous being. How dare Jeremy attack her—and for what? To feel like a big man? What an affront. Imagine a world so small that your ego can fill all of it.

When Renee ran to the tower with the now-pummeled playboy, she thought she was hurtling toward uncertainty. She was ready for an end, an abyss. She wasn't expecting to find this magnificent being, waiting for her on the other side of the darkness. There is a brutal majesty to her, a concreteness, a reassuring physicality. She is a vision of life differently ordered.

Almost unconsciously, Renee takes a step toward her. Even sitting down, resting against the rock behind her, the ape lady comes up to her chest.

This isn't the first time she has had to ward trespassers off her mountaintop, Renee feels certain. Because this place is clearly hers. The stone observatory is her jungle gym, the cave is her home, and the trees are her hiding places, endless and lush. The light of the sun rising beyond the stone tower brings a seemingly infinite string of islands into view, scattered across the sea below them, gray shapes that become green jewels as the dawn begins to break, casting the tower's long shadow across the clearing. All of this belongs to her, doesn't it?

Yes.

Renee takes another step toward her, only a few feet away now, and the ape grunts in reply. A warning.

"It's OK," Renee says, holding out her hands to show she's not a threat.

Renee looks down at the creature's ancient eyes. They're the color of wheat—from an overgrown field that has crisped for too long on summer days. Although she is wincing in pain, she regards Renee with a keen, almost human awareness—or perhaps a superhuman one. She may not speak but she holds in those eyes lifetimes Renee has never experienced, could never experience.

"It's OK," Renee assures her again, bending at the knees.

And then Renee is eye level with her, the beast evincing a kind of cautious trust. Her fur is long and scraggly, with little burs and bristles caught in the hairs. Those can be brushed out later; it's the gash on her arm that needs care right now. It's not a long cut, but it is deep, gurgling blood that mats down the fur around it, coloring it sickly shades of crimson and black. So long as Renee can stop the bleeding, she will be all right.

As Renee assesses the situation, a dead Jeremy stares vacantly at her from the corner of her vision, a piece of his brain visible through a crack in his skull. Renee reaches out to brusquely roll his head the other direction, so that he won't distract her from her work.

That's better.

Jeremy has looked at her enough. He can stop now.

She easily peels Jeremy's fingers off the rock in his hand, his grip not yet stiffened by rigor mortis, and hears the lady ape grunt. In fear? How else can Renee interpret the widening of her eyes? The quickening of her breath?

"No, no, no, I'm helping," Renee says, holding up her free hand, then pointedly stretching out the bottom of her white undershirt.

She uses the jagged edge to tear off long strips of the white fabric, leaving her stomach exposed to the air, but the sun will warm them both soon enough. After carefully setting the rock back down on the ground, Renee scoots closer to the beast. "See?" she assures, and although there's no reply, the being seems to understand the pacific gesture.

She holds a long strip of the undershirt taut and presses the middle of it to the lady ape's wound, the fabric instantly absorbing a small spurt of blood. Renee carefully reaches around the wounded arm to wrap and tie the ends of the undershirt together. The ape-woman is soft, Renee notices, as her hand brushes against her dense fur. All the while, the beautiful creature looks at Renee with hesitation, but undeniable gratitude. Hopefully the blood will coagulate soon.

"You'll be OK," Renee says, confident that she can sense her meaning. "Everything is going to be OK."

Footsteps slap against the stone somewhere in the expanse behind her, and Renee is momentarily unmoored from the almost meditative state she has entered. In an instant, Renee prepares to leap up and defend her from a *Catch* producer or explain the situation to an early-bird hiker. But when she stands up and whips around, she sees someone that some corner of her mind was almost expecting to find here: a woman with hair as silver as the morning, striding across the clearing with an alacrity that belies her age.

Margaret Davies.

"Renee," Maggie says, as she draws closer.

"Margaret?"

"Just call me Maggie, remember?"

"Right," Renee says, "Maggie."

Maggie does not seem surprised to find Renee tending to a lady Sasquatch at the crack of dawn, nor is she disturbed by the gruesome tableau of bodies—Lilah-Mae's, Vanessa's, and Jeremy's—in various states of disrepair. Instead, Maggie looks past Renee at the ape with the same deep concern in her eyes that Renee felt well up inside her minutes ago when she saw her injury.

"How is she doing?" Maggie asks. Renee knows that Maggie understands this wounded creature, and Maggie knows she doesn't need to explain it to her. Maybe she would have yesterday, but not today.

"I think I stopped the bleeding," Renee informs her, pointing at her makeshift wound dressing.

"You did a good job," Maggie says, squinting to examine Renee's handiwork. "She'll be OK. She's survived worse."

"How old is she?" Renee asks. "Where did she come from?"

"We don't know. Kathy always liked to say that she swam here a long time ago. That she went out looking for a place of her own, just like we did. But that was probably just a sweet thought. That was so like Kathy. Ever the romantic."

Below them both, the Sasquatch gazes upward, her expression calm now, the acuteness of her pain subsiding. Her coffee-colored fur ripples for a few seconds under a light breeze. Renee pauses and thinks for a moment, trying to imagine what she's feeling behind her ancient eyes.

Maggie bends slightly to stroke the beast on her good arm. "She wants companionship, same as you or I, she just has a funny way of going about getting it—and she gets grumpy if it's been too long since she's made new friends." At that, Maggie gestures toward Lilah-Mae's body hanging in the tree. "She has her own logic that we try to understand and adapt to. Otters is hers, after all."

Renee leans down alongside Maggie and although this ought to be the weirdest moment of her life, tending to this legendary being with a septuagenarian innkeeper feels like a homecoming. How strange eyes are that they can capture this scene. Two squishy little orbs of nerves and jelly: indelible things that alter all the rest of you. Renee can't imagine going back to . . . what? Tampa? And leave *this* behind?

The Sasquatch huffs contentedly as Maggie runs a delicate hand from the crown of her head down to her shoulder, then along her arm to her wrist, before grabbing a hairy hand and taking it in her own, wrinkled fingers interlacing with furry ones.

"You're OK now, aren't you, Patricia?" Maggie coos.

"Patricia." Renee tries out the name on her tongue. It has a hint of whimsy to it, but it's timeless, too, in a way—just like her. "She's beautiful, isn't she?"

"Yes. She's beautiful."

Renee reaches out and strokes Patricia's fur, head to chin, head to chin.

CatchChat.com

TRexDerickson • 9.21.19 • 12:35 PM

Hey, Catchers. By now, you've all seen the sad news. The media got to the story before I did, but I can fill in some details the other outlets won't share—if only because I think it will help us all make sense of this terrible tragedy.

First, though, a confent warning: the new information I have to share is graphic.

Here's what we already know: Dex Derickson, the host of *The Catch*, died late Thursday night in an apparent drunk-driving accident. Amanda Parker, Vanessa Voorhees, Lilah-Mae Adams, and Renee Irons are all missing, as is Jeremy Blackstone. A photo leaked to the press—please don't repost it here if you've seen it— showed another man dead, apparently from a self-inflicted gunshot wound, near a lake midway up Mount Resilience, where the final Date Night took place.

I can now confirm via my source that the man in this photo was a crew member by the name of Mike Chan. What wasn't shown in that leaked photo—thank God—was longtime producer Casey Collins, lying near Chan's body, after she was apparently drowned. Based on forensic evidence, police strongly suspect some kind of murder-suicide/spree-killing scenario. The surviving crew are all shocked. They say Mike was an easygoing guy who liked working on the show. But my source did mention Mike having a thing for Casey, possibly unrequited—and sadly we all know how those situations can end.

I suspect we'll find out more in the coming days and weeks, as searches continue for the missing girls and for Jeremy Blackstone. I'll bring you more information about any of the others as soon as I can.

For now, I think all we can do is send thoughts and prayers to everyone experiencing a loss right now, both the producers and the families of the missing contestants.

○ **CatcherInTheSky** • 9.21.19 • 12:40 PM

Oh my God. My heart goes out to everyone involved: to the cast, the crew, and their families. I can't imagine what they're going through. What an unspeakable loss.

○ **GlamstaRicks** • 9.21.19 • 12:42 PM

It's always the "nice" ones, isn't it? Every time one of these guys shoots up their workplace, all the headlines are about how "quiet" he was or about how "friendly" he seemed, and how they *never* expected he'd be the type to do something like this. It's time to quit carrying water for killers like this Chan guy. I don't care how many puppies he saved before he went homicidal.

○ **DexIsMyZaddy** • 9.21.19 • 12:45 PM

Don't hate me for asking this, but I take it we're not going to get to see any of this season? Not even a shortened version? Do we think *The Catch* will be canceled?

○ **CatcherInTheSky** • 9.21.19 • 12:47 PM

Seriously?! You are sick. Their bodies aren't even in the ground yet. The cast might still be in the woods, fighting to survive. And you're worried about the show? Mods, can we delete this post?

○ **CatchMeIfYouCan · 9.21.20 · 12:49 PM**

I don't think we'll see any footage from this season, but I fully expect there to be a true-crime documentary about this someday. I think it could be done in a sensitive way that honors the victims. If the cast members are all dead—God forbid—they'd want a light to be shined on their final moments, wouldn't they? It would actually be more disrespectful, I think, to throw away the last two months of their lives.

○ **TRexDerickson · 9.21.20 · 12:52 PM**

I can confirm that there have already been early internal talks at the network about producing an hourlong documentary special to commemorate Dex and to honor the fallen crew while searches for the contestants continue.

Stay tuned.

The hat Laurel Quinn is looking at is expensive but cute—braided straw with a topaz-blue fabric band—and besides, it's not like this store has any other options. A sudden gust of wind on the ferry's observation deck claimed the one she was planning to wear during this Otters Island getaway with the girls. Right now, it's swimming somewhere near the bottom of the Salish Sea, where there's probably an entire underwater mountain of lost scarves and sunglasses.

So this particular hat, the most fashionable piece of apparel in this small outdoors shop—mostly by default—will have to do.

Laurel carries it to the counter by its brim, passing wrought-iron racks filled with hiking equipment, protein bars, and powder-coated thermos bottles. A woman in her fifties stands behind the counter. She smiles reassuringly at Laurel as she approaches the register and sets the hat down beside a dusty carousel of brochures: "Salish Shelters," one of them says, and then in all caps: "CAMPING WITH CLASS."

"Will that be all for you?" the cashier asks.

"Yup," Laurel says, shifting her gaze away from the brochure, and noticing the woman's face for the first time. She looks familiar, though Laurel can't quite place her.

"That'll be $69.99."

It's a rip-off but Laurel dutifully begins entering her PIN into her watch to open up her barcode.

"First time on Otters?" the woman asks.

"Yeah," Laurel says, looking up. Her finger slips on the last digit of her PIN. She huffs and starts from the beginning.

"Well then, welcome to the island," the woman says, unmoved by the minor drama playing out between Laurel and her smart watch.

The woman speaks in an unhurried way. As if she has been standing right here behind this very counter, selling exactly these hats every year for the last forever, totally uninterested in life outside Otters. Then again, there's something a little off with almost anyone who still works in retail in 2044. It's almost always in remote places like this that stores still need to be manned. It would be easier to just buy the hat from a locker, but Laurel supposes it's good to support a vintage, woman-owned small business.

She finishes entering her PIN, but now the clerk is fiddling with her code reader, trying to get it to start.

As she does, Laurel remembers who the cashier reminds her of: she looks distractingly like that Renee woman from the Netflix docuseries about the *Catch* tragedy, but a bit older, the lines beneath her eyes more pronounced. They tried to keep that dating show going for a few years after all those people died. Laurel never saw any of it, but her mom used to watch it every week with her friends.

"I'm sure you get this a lot," Laurel says, after debating for a second about whether to bring it up, "but have you seen *The Last Corsage* on Netflix?"

The woman laughs as she whips open a large paper bag, before returning her attention to the code reader.

"I *do* get it a lot," she says, the corners of her mouth crinkling in a smile. "I'm not her, but I'll take the compliment."

The woman issues a small smile of triumph as the code reader blinks to life. She extends it toward Laurel, who holds out her wrist to pay for the hat, wincing at the thought that a gust of wind on the ferry is now costing her as much as brunch will tomorrow. The girls have already picked out a cute place in West Bay: Mary's. Bottomless mimosas, eggs Benedict, yum.

Shit.

Did she remember to tell Sadie that she wants her London Fog latte iced, not hot? The girls are picking up coffee across the street while Laurel replaces her hat.

"Mainly we're happy the show is sending business our way," the woman continues. "But it was also pretty silly."

"Yeah," Laurel admits. "A lot of it felt like a reach. Especially when they started digging up those old blog posts from that Abigail woman. The one who thought Bigfoot's sister lived out here or something."

The woman laughs again, stuffing the hat into the oversized crinkly paper bag. "Do you need a receipt?" she asks.

"No thanks," Laurel says, tapping her watch. "I got it on here."

Laurel's dad once showed her a meme about a pharmacy that had infamously long receipts, like twelve inches long for a single pack of gum. He seemed almost nostalgic for it.

Laurel grabs the bag from the counter and turns, heading toward the sunlight waiting for her on the other side of the glass-paned door.

"Sorry, just one more question," Laurel says. "My friends and I want to go camping one night this week. Make some s'mores. Wake up to a view. Do you have any recommendations?"

The woman smiles.

"Well, if you're not afraid of lady Bigfoot," she says, pulling out one of the dusty brochures from the countertop display, "I know the perfect spot."

Behind the Scenes
Protector Chat

PLANNING

August 15, 2019

Brittany Horton: Can't we do this on a text chain? I had to reset my password twice today. 10:00 AM

Abigail Choi: You ABSOLUTELY cannot text ANYONE about this. Secrecy is sacred. Using this secure application is the only way to ensure our communications are encrypted. 10:01 AM

Mary Dunlap: Don't you mean en-*cryptid*? 10:01 AM

Allison Graves: I'm voting you off the island lol 10:01 AM

Abigail Choi: Patricia's safety isn't a joke. Mainland whispers are one thing, but She could be captured or killed if you leave an actual digital trail. 10:02 AM

Mary Dunlap: Didn't you just move here, like, two seconds ago? Relax. We know the rules. 10:02 AM

Abigail Choi: I've been here since 2004, Mary, and need I remind you that I'm the president of the planning subcommittee? This will be the most activity we've seen on Mount Resilience in years. There's too much on the line for us to goof around. 10:03 AM

Brittany Horton: I know we voted already but I still think this plan is overkill. Haven't we only seen one dead sheep? 10:04 AM

Margaret Davies: ABIGAIL IS RIGHT. US GOLDEN-AGERS CAN FEEL HER MOODS IN THE AIR. PATRICIA NEEDS A CERTAIN CADENCE TO HER COMPANY. WE'RE IN DIRE STRAITS. AND THAT ONE DEAD SHEEP RUINED MY DECK. SINCERELY, MAGGIE 10:06 AM

Mary Dunlap: Maggie, please turn your Caps Lock off. And you don't need to sign your messages. These aren't letters. 10:06 AM

SEPTEMBER 12, 2019

Mary Dunlap: This plan better work. I just got the breakfast order from the crew. I'm not sure there's enough flour on the island to feed them. 2:38 PM

Margaret Davies: At least you're not housing anyone. 😄 2:39 PM

Allison Graves: Maggie, was that an emoji? You're really getting the hang of this! 2:39 PM

Margaret Davies: I had to learn Glamstapix to market the B and B. I can learn this for Patricia. 🌑 🙄 🎞 2:40 PM

Mary Dunlap: At least you're getting paid, Maggie. The contract Abby made me sign said I'd provide free craft services in exchange for an "establishing shot" of the bakery. 2:41 PM

Abigail Choi: We're all giving a lot. Brittany is providing the yurts for free, too. But we have to look at the bigger picture. Ensuring Patricia has what She needs is more important than any of us making money. 2:42 PM

Brittany Horton: And no one's worried about something bad happening to Patricia? 2:43 PM

Margaret Davies: She's a salty old gal. She'll be all right, Brittany. Even if some of those TV people leave here with tall tales, no authorities are going to believe them. 2:44 PM

Abigail Choi: Exactly. And if anyone does threaten Her, that's what we're here for. 2:44 PM

Mary Dunlap: Now, that we can agree on. No one's hurting our girl. Not on my watch. 2:45 PM

Margaret Davies: 🫖 2:45 PM

Allison Graves: OK, seriously, Maggie. Did you memorize every emoji? 2:46 PM

OPERATIONS

SEPTEMBER 19, 2019

Mitchell Jackson: Good morning, all! Just wanted to make sure everything's in motion. Maggie, the cast made it to your place in one piece? 8:59 AM

Margaret Davies: I've got a full 🏠. 9:00 AM

Mitchell Jackson: Mary, the observation team is prepped? 9:01 AM

Mary Dunlap: Yes, sir. I made fifty ham and Swiss croissants this morning and still had time to clean my guns. 9:02 AM

Mitchell Jackson: You truly contain multitudes. Any other updates? 9:02 AM

Margaret Davies: Yes. One of the TV girls seems like she could be one of us. Renee. She's searching for something, I can tell. But I suppose we'll let Patricia decide. 9:03 AM

Mitchell Jackson: Indeed we shall, Maggie dear. Thanks, everyone. I've got a helicopter to fly in a few, so I'm off! More soon. 9:03 AM

Mitchell Jackson: Anybody got any Windex? 11:17 AM

SEPTEMBER 20, 2019

Mitchell Jackson: Was that a gunshot? 2:04 AM

Marci Cummings: I heard it, too. What's going on up there? 2:04 AM

Brittany Horton: Is Patricia OK? 2:04 AM

Abigail Choi: Gunshot was us. 2:05 AM

Marci Cummings: Wait, what?! "Observe don't obstruct." That's Otters 101, you bumbling fools! 2:05 AM

Abigail Choi: Please calm down, Marci. I'll update everyone soon. 2:06 AM

Marci Cummings: I thought you said the host was dead when you found him. 2:07 AM

Mitchell Jackson: That's it, I'm going up there. 2:10 AM

Abigail Choi: No need. We've got it under control. 2:11 AM

Jacqueline Maldonado: Sorry. I can fill everyone in while Mary and Abby handle this. 2:11 AM

Marci Cummings: Type faster, Jacky. 2:14 AM

Jacqueline Maldonado: Maggie left footprints from the wreck and a camera guy followed them. We shot him when he caught us and we're taking care of the girl with him now. 2:17 AM

Marci Cummings: Damn it. Isn't it past batty old Maggie's bedtime? 2:17 AM

Mitchell Jackson: Maggie and Kathy have done more for Patricia and Otters than any of us. I know you're stressed, Marci, but this isn't the time to lose our cool. 2:18 AM

Brittany Horton: I'm just glad Patricia's safe. 2:18 AM

Marci Cummings left the channel.

Mitchell Jackson: Well, this is messier than I would have liked, but it seems containable. I'll give Sheriff Shannon a ring and let her know we've got some bodies to stage. 2:20 AM

Mitchell Jackson: Good morning. I know it was a long night. How are we doing? 9:03 AM

Mary Dunlap: I'm a little peeved. One of the producers called to ask why breakfast was late. I wonder if cyanide changes the taste of kouign-amann. 9:04 AM

Mitchell Jackson: Let's not make Shan's job harder than it already is. 9:04 AM

Brittany Horton: How is Patricia? 9:05 AM

Margaret Davies: Patricia is just fine. She's resting now. Thanks to Renee.
9:05 AM

DIRECT MESSAGE

APRIL 15, 2020

Margaret Davies: Thanks for doing this online, Renee. I typically like to have these orientations in person but I suppose I'm "high-risk." How is Mary's guesthouse treating you? 1:15 PM

Renee Irons: Her pastries aren't as yummy as yours but other than that, it's lovely. Being here while the world collapses around us—I feel like I escaped in the nick of time. Plus, the shower doesn't clog with a dozen other girls' hair every day. 1:16 PM

Margaret Davies: That's sweet of you to say. About the pastries, I mean. Any questions? Reservations? 1:17 PM

Renee Irons: I just want to know more about Patricia's past. Dig into the archives. 1:18 PM

Margaret Davies: A lot of it is murky, even to me. We know the first women to call themselves Protectors were part of a sewing circle in the 1880s. Records get spottier during the wars. Kathy was the history buff. But you can go through that dusty box of loose papers yourself after this. 1:20 PM

Renee Irons: Do they mention anything about others out there? Like Her?
1:20 PM

Margaret Davies: Not that we know of, but everyone has their theories. Abigail believes Patricia is the last of Her kind. If you get Marci going, she'll talk nonsense about parallel timelines. But me? I'm certain there are others. She couldn't have come from nothing. 1:22 PM

Renee Irons: I hope She lives forever. 1:24 PM

Margaret Davies: Maybe She will. 💜 1:24 PM

Acknowledgments

No book as weird as this one sees the light of day without a team of weirdos who believes in it. Thank you, above all, to Sareena Kamath at Zando, who connected with *Patricia* early on, then vigorously massaged and restructured it until her exacting standards were met. Sareena, you're a beautiful genius. You get my first corsage, my last corsage, and every petal of every flower between them.

Undying thanks to Leila Campoli, my agent at Stonesong, who bore with me after I came up with some more grounded book ideas, only to toss them aside and email her, "I think I might be losing my mind, but here's what I'm working on now . . ." You are a better advocate for my books than I deserve and the best first reader in the business.

Jacob Tobia, your friendship is the reason I kept going when I felt like giving up, and the reason Patricia is who she ended up becoming. You encouraged me to be my strangest, most honest self and to pursue my wildest whims instead of posturing for the cool kids.

I'm grateful to Sharon and Ryan McIlvain, who spent a holiday weekend flying through the book, giving feedback, and soothing my anxieties. Likewise, to Rayna Berggren, Jennifer Culp, and Sadie Collins, who provided crucial notes on early drafts. Evan, your laughter at the lines that were meant to be funny was tremendously reassuring.

My wife, Corey, Kathy to my Maggie, told me to do something that would scare me and that would stretch my abilities. She said to write the kind of book I always dreamed of writing, not the one I already knew I could. I love you, big boo, and hope I've done you proud. You'll always be my final girl.

Amanda Zimlich at Otters Pond Bed & Breakfast on Orcas Island made the choice of setting for this book obvious from the beginning. Thank you, chef, for introducing me to the full splendor of the San Juans—and for the omelets.

And a final word for Zuma, my beloved sphynx cat, who sadly passed away as I was completing this novel: You can't read this because you are a cat—although who knows what abilities you gained in kitty heaven?—but you are in this book, too, you woefully misunderstood creature, you. I would have started a death cult for you.